The Cell

By

Joshua L.A. Jones

Edited by Mark Frankel

The Cell

Published by Aegis Creative Enterprises
Copyright 2012

Joshua L.A. Jones
The Cell: first edition

Other books by this author include: The Excess Road, Whispers of
Hypnos, Blue lips and crayons, Santa's a Zombie? and
Oneiromancer.

For more information on the author please go to
http://aegispub.blogspot.com or follow him on Twitter @JLAJones

Dedication:

I'd like to thank Mark Frankel for being my friend first and editor second. Without his help this novel would never have made it off the ground. I'd also like to thank C.B. Cebulski for his insight into the world of comic books and inspiring me to pursue the underlying themes within the subtext. Thank you to Zack Rosenberg for thinking this project might actually be something good and the support to help push the story along. Finally, thanks to my mother who allowed me to be me and to everyone out there who reads independent writers. You all rock. Ars longa, vitae brevis.

Chapter 1: The calling

In the back of the classroom, Les Logan opened a yellow folder on his desk and pulled out an unfinished comic book page from a stack of sketches. His friend Aki who was sitting next to him saw this and shook his head in protest. Les faced Aki and then pointed to the front of the room where a newspaper stretched across the teacher's face like a sail tight with wind.

A quick nod from Aki signaled that he would join in the fun. Les passed the page across the aisle, but it slipped from Aki's hand, and spun like a helicopter blade to the floor. Les bent over to swipe the paper off the ground but caught his elbow on the corner of the desk and a bang ricocheted off the walls of the study-hall.

The newspaper folded down to reveal Mr. Pym's sunken eyes. Above them, eyebrows as white as chalk crawled across his brow like a furry caterpillar. The teacher stared at Les as he tried to sit back in his seat and look like nothing happened.

"Mr. Logan, I should have suspected as much," Mr. Pym said, put the newspaper down flat, and stood.

The teacher's head tilted with a curious look as he clasped his hands behind his back and walked down the rows of desks with a slight waddle. Each student froze as he passed. Mr. Pym then stood before Les and pointed to his desk.

"What sort of contraband is that?" Mr. Pym asked.

Les looked up to Mr. Pym with wide eyes and spun the dial on his watch.

"It's not contraband. It's graphic design homework Mr. Pym. Me and Aki teamed up on a project," Les said. Out of the corner of his eye, he could see the fear streak across Aki's face.

"Oh, is that so? Fine. You are both allowed to work on the project together. Quietly," Mr. Pym said, scanned the classroom, and continued, "but as for the rest, you will be silent."

With a slow pivot, Mr. Pym began to walk back up to his desk and Les leaned across the aisle and poked Aki's shoulder. As the teacher sat down, Aki spun to look Les right in the eyes.

"Dude, can't believe he bought it," Les said.

"Me neither. If my parents find out I'm working on comics in class, I'm dead," Aki said.

"Me too," Les said as Aki smiled.

"But since we have permission, let's work on Ectomancer the Angel Eater," Aki said.

They pushed their desks together, pulled out pens, and spread the pages across both desks. Les grinned a devious grin and spun the dial on his watch.

"If we use study-hall to work on Ectomancer, we'll have it ready for the New York ComicCon for sure," Les said.

"First you have to figure out the ending and I have to finish the page layouts. Can't impress comic editors at the con with unfinished work," Aki said.

"I do get to draw some, right?" Les asked.

"Of course, we're partners."

After last period, Les and Aki lugged their overstuffed backpacks down Reed Hall through the scurrying tide of sophomores and freshman heading towards the buses parked on the west campus lot. Being juniors, they naturally headed towards the back parking lot where the bright yellow buses never held court. Then, in the middle of the hallway, Les stopped in his tracks as he remembered something and the flow of underclassmen diverted around him. Aki saw and hiked up his backpack as he turned to face Les.

"What's up?" Aki asked.

"Forgot my chemistry book. Wait for me, I'll be right back. Just going to my locker," Les said.

"Hurry dude, I think snow is falling."

As the halls cleared, Les was able to pick up the pace and passed by the trophy case where a large photo of the hockey team that won the conference championship sat under a flickering overhead light. He gave it a glance but nothing more. At that moment, just as Les was about to round the corner, he heard a metallic crunch as if someone had been slammed into the lockers. Les made the bend and looked down the empty hall to see that someone had indeed been slammed into the lockers by Gint and the Goon, the baby-face brothers. They were the town bullies who wore only denim since elementary school.

Even though Les was pretty stout for a seventeen year old, fear began to make him sweat because Goon was more Mastodon than man. His older brother Gint with his ratty hair and rail thin arms controlled his every move. Goon had a wiry freshman named

Grayson pinned to the lockers and the kid was struggling to pull a handful of singles out of his pocket. Les figured it might get worse if he interfered so he walked up to his locker and hoped a teacher would pop out through one of the classroom doors.

"You know kid, if you didn't wear those dorky clothes you wouldn't be a target," Gint said.

"Fag," Goon said and chuckled.

The word didn't sit well with Les and he stopped rotating the combination lock. Fear was replaced with anger that launched down his spine. The hot stings of adrenaline jabbed at his back and his hands began to tremble. Even though Les knew he might get pummeled, he slipped off the backpack heavy with books and dragged it one-armed across the floor toward the brothers. He locked his eyes on Gint as he approached. Gint turned to see Les and smirked.

"What do you want Leslie?" Gint asked.

Les rushed forward, spun, and swept his backpack across the floor and took Goon's legs out from under him. Gint froze as his towering brother fell to the floor like a clumsy elephant. In a flash, Les had Gint in a headlock as Goon tried to get up off his back.

"Go," Les said to Grayson.

"Thanks Les," Grayson said and fled down the hall.

Gint squirmed and then flailed his arms in an attempt to punch Les so he tightened his hold.

"No one's afraid of you anymore. Cool it, or next time, you guys are getting jacked. And not just by me," Les said and released his hold. Gint slipped down to the ground and began to cough.

Les picked up his backpack as Goon was lumbering up to one knee. Without looking like he was running scared, Les took off down the hall.

Looking a bit flushed, Les found Aki just where he had left him leaned up against the wall checking emails on his phone. Aki looked at Les and a curl of confusion wrinkled his face.

"You good?" Aki asked.

"Yeah dude. Didn't get my book but I'm good. I can just get the notes online."

As the winter wind swirled across the campus, they walked to the far end of New Hebron High's back parking lot and hopped into Aki's silver Honda Civic that was covered in a light dusting of snow.

"Dude, let's go downtown before heading home. I want to show you a new sketch," Les said.

"Cool, we need to discuss the plan for going to the New York ComicCon too and can't do it around the folks," Aki said.

They drove down the narrow streets and passed by rows of snow covered lawns until they reached the downtown section of the Connecticut hamlet. Holiday lights strung up on brick-face storefronts cut through the gray overcast that had rolled in from the south. They pulled into the rundown 7-11 on the corner of Parker Street and Jordan Drive. When Aki put the car in park, Les turned and tapped his friend's shoulder.

"Hold on. I'm getting nachos," Les said with an impish grin.

"Fine," Aki said and shook his head.

"Oops almost forgot," Les said.

He unzipped the backpack at his feet, pulled out a folder, and flipped it open to reveal a sketch. He handed the drawing to Aki.

"Interesting," Aki said.

Les opened the door, the chill bellowed in, and he got out of the car as he popped the hood of his gray sweatshirt over his head. With slow steps, he made his way to the sliding glass door being careful to avoid the patches of ice on the ground that formed below the dripping gutters. In just a few moments, Les was standing at the register with an overflowing container of nachos. His impish grin had become a full blown demonic smile as he paid the clerk.

The scent of chili and cheese from the convenience store nachos ballooned through the interior as Aki examined the sketch of a dark-elf figure. In the passenger seat, Les dipped a chip into the yellow cheese sauce as he waited for Aki's opinion.

"Dude, those nachos are vile," Aki said.

"No, that wasabi at dinner last night was vile," Les said, held the chip high and then crunched down.

"At least wasabi is real. Not like that plastic cheese," Aki said and shook his head.

A black BMW 5 series parked in the next spot and Les saw Vicky Price, a senior in his Trigonometry class, take her keys out of the ignition. He shot Aki a quick upward nod.

"Dude it's Vicky. Heard she likes younger guys. Show her your game man," Les said.

"She only hooks up with jocks and probably isn't into Japanese guys," Aki said and lowered the sketch to reveal the eyes that no one in New Hebron had besides his parents.

"Fine," Les said, handed the warm plastic container of nachos to Aki, and got out of the car just as Vicky closed her door with a flat thud. She flipped back her long black hair and then checked her beige Channel purse that hung like a pendulum under her arm. Her frozen breath drifted away on the sharp winter breeze as Les zipped up his sweatshirt.

A short wave got her attention as Les made his way around the front of the car and avoided the snowmelt dripping off the store's roof. The worn soles of his Adidas slipped as he stepped on a dark patch of ice but he never lost his balance.

"What's up Vicky?" Les asked and put his hands in his jean pockets.

"Hey Les. Just getting a Redbull before I go up to the lot at Sturges Park. You should go. There's like fifty people up there," she said.

"That's up by the reservoir?" he asked. A phone buzzed inside her purse and she plucked it out with manicured fingernails.

"Right. Got to take this. See you there," she said and began to read a text as she walked up to the automatic glass door that opened with an electric whoosh. Les hopped back inside the car and Aki held out the nachos.

"Take these before I toss them out the window," Aki said.

Les grabbed the plastic container and sat back with a devilish smile.

"Vicky said there are tons of people up at Sturges. Let's go," Les said as he dipped a chip in the shiny yellow cheese sauce.

"I don't know. The roads are slippery. Plus we need to discuss going to the New York con," Aki said.

"Dude, come on. Hot girls to scope," Les said.

"Not like any want to date a geek like me," Aki said.

"You never know if you don't try. Hey, you didn't want to go that Rangers' game at MSG but you went and liked it," Les said and spun the dial on his watch.

"That's different. The Rangers weren't going to tell me to get lost," Aki said.

"Didn't you tell me to try new things when I didn't want to go to the con in Stamford?" Les asked and spun the dial to his watch.

"Yeah but that's different," Aki said.

"How?" Les asked and spun the dial.

"In every way. Dude, what's with the watch thing? You're like the only person who wears a watch anymore and you spin that dial like every five minutes," Aki said with an annoyed glare.

"If we go, I'll tell you. Okay?"

"Tell me and maybe."

"It's my grandfather's. Before he died, he gave it to me when my dad was giving me a hard time about quitting sports. He said I could do what want if I put in the time. So when I get anxious, I spin the dial and it makes me feel better," Les said.

"You spin that dial a lot," Aki said.

"Yeah, but I don't let fear stop me from doing new things," Les said.

Outside, Vicky waved to them as she walked by and got back into her car. Les looked at Aki and raised an eyebrow.

"All right, but if it starts snowing I'm turning around," Aki said and handed Les the elf sketch.

"Cool."

In about ten minutes, Aki's car reached the outskirts of town as the landscape bulged upward to the hills spiked with bare trees. The road narrowed as it snaked through the woods surrounding the reservoir. Les grew impatient since Aki was driving slow and never said anything about his drawing. He spun the dial on his watch as he shot Aki a glance.

"Dude, so how was the elf?" Les asked.

"Uh it was really good Les. You're getting the proportions right, but just like I told you before, you need to focus on the hands a little more," Aki said.

"I know. Just get a little rushed sometimes, I need to slow down like you said," Les replied as he sat deep in his seat.

They entered a stretch of hanging mist that froze as it coated his windshield. Aki clicked on the windshield wipers and tapped the defrost button. Hot air gushed from the vents with a low hiss as the wiper blades skimmed back and forth with a rhythmic swish. Les looked at clock on the dash.

"Hurry up. You drive like an old lady Aki. By the time we get there, they'll be gone," Les said.

"Driving as fast as I can. By the way, since we're sharing, what do you really think of Ectomancer?" Aki asked.

"Hey man it's a cool concept but it's kind of outside of what I read. I mean paranormal stuff with angels, ghost sorcerers and the afterlife is cool but I really don't know a lot about it. That's why I think it's so hard for me to plot out an ending," Les said.

Outside on the windshield, sleet began to ding and Aki's knuckles stretched his skin white as he clenched the steering wheel.

"That's what I thought. Man, I hate this cold weather," Aki said.

"It's just a little sleet. So how did you come up with Ziggy Helm, the Ectomancer, the ghost who eats angels?" Les asked.

The car slowed as Aki depressed the gas pedal as they reached a bend in the road.

"Saw a show on Discovery that talked about how matter and energy can't be destroyed. It can only change and that got me thinking that maybe there is something more than just this life. Dying might just be a transformation of energy," Aki said.

"Maybe, but you know what, I'll deal with death when I'm dead," Les said.

"Might be too late then," Aki said.

"Then I'll come back and haunt you," Les said with chuckle.

"And do what? Knock some plates over, scare my cat?"

"No, since you don't like the cold, I'll cover you with cold spots like the spirits do on those ghost hunter shows," Les said.

"So you'd be a dick from beyond the grave?"

"Yup. Now hurry up. All the girls are going to be gone," Les said.

Coming up, Les could see the stoplight blinking yellow at the crossroads of Evergreen Lane and King's Highway. Aki pressed the breaks as they approached but the car slid on a patch of black ice and went right into the intersection. At that moment, time became slow and thick like cold honey running down a spoon as Les turned towards Aki and saw the headlights of a white Chevy Suburban beam through the window.

Dense blue smoke drifted through the surrounding forest as sleet began to fall like shattered glass. Les's watch spun in the middle of the road and when it came to a stop, the hour and minute hands did too.

Chapter 2: Recall.

8:00 AM

June 30th

Les sat stiff in the back of his father's Nissan sedan as he prepared to deliver a speech. The windows were shut to keep out the noise despite the eighty degree heat. Sweat gloved his shaky hands and wouldn't dry no matter how many times he wiped them on the upholstery. Les tugged on the collar of his white shirt as he twisted his neck. His cheeks puffed as he exhaled through tight pressed lips.

"Don't want to do this," he said, folded his speech, and put it in his shirt pocket.

Through the windows Les surveyed the parking lot that curled around the town hall. Most spots were crammed with SUV's donning honor roll bumper stickers that bent up at the edges from the summer heat.

"Need to relax," he said.

He sat back, shoulders locked, and began to check the messages in his cell phone. Les shook his head as he hit the keypad.

"Hate this phone."

A mass of chilly air rolled across Les like a dense fog over a warm New England bay. He sat up and scanned the dashboard to see if the AC was somehow turned on. It wasn't. His face wrinkled with confusion. The last time he felt cold was that the day of the accident.

"Why am I freezing?" he asked.

The chill crept out of the car a second later and Les scratched his head.

"Weird."

Back to his task, a number that shouldn't have called caught Les's attention in his recent call log. His hands trembled even more than before.

Is that Aki's old number? Couldn't be, Les thought.

Outside, knuckles like steel rivets tapped on the window and Les turned to see his father's square face, worn by worry, looking back at him. He waved his father into the car. Mr. Logan wrenched the front passenger door open with a mighty tug and the humid air bellowed in as he sat down. The door closed with a round thud.

"Okay Les, you have about five minutes until Principle Wayne is done," Mr. Logan said and looked back at his son.

"Can't do it Dad. Will you do it for me?" Les asked.

"No Les. You'll do fine. It's all right to be scared," Mr. Logan said.

"I'll mess it up," Les said.

"Do you have your speech?" Mr. Logan asked.

"Yes," Les said and patted his right pocket.

"Good. Just take a deep breath and read it slow. You'll do fine," Mr. Logan said.

"But Dad, I can't stop shaking," Les said.

"It's okay Les. Everything's ready," Mr. Logan said.

Les began to scratch his knee through his khaki pants. Mr. Logan reached over and grabbed his son's hand. It was cold, too cold for such a warm day.

"No one is here to judge you. We're here to remember Aki. Let's go," Mr. Logan said and exited the car.

Still curious, Les looked at his phone but the number had vanished from the screen. He shrugged, took a deep breath, and closed his eyes as he exhaled. His eyes opened and he glanced over at the crowd.

"Just do it," Les said.

The piece of notebook paper with a speech scribbled in pencil clung to the inside of his shirt pocket but it let go with a decisive tug. Les slid the old flip phone inside his pant's pocket and hopped out into the clear morning. Mr. Logan put his arm around Les's shoulders and they walked towards the town green that spread flat like a football field before him. A white gazebo that was draped in sheets of morning sunlight stood where three cobblestone sidewalks met in the center of the lawn. Next to it, Principle Wayne addressed a crowd dressed in their Sunday best even though it was Saturday.

The sidewalk clacked under the soles of Les's black wingtips and his forehead began to sweat as he headed towards the gathering. The scent of freshly cut grass rose up to Les's nose and he almost sneezed but with a couple strong sniffles he held it back.

He wiped his brow with the sleeve of his shirt and looked down to the ground as he walked.

Mr. Logan and Les reached the edge of the crowd where his mother was waiting with a sorrowful look on her face. She fixed Les's hair with a few quick strokes of her long fingers and kissed his cheek. Principle Wayne, dressed in a black suit, ended his commemoration of Aki Kubo with a smile.

Principle Wayne introduced Les as Lester Logan and stepped behind the dogwood sapling resting on the blades of a hand truck that was parked at the edge of a hole in the lawn. The root ball of the sapling was bundled with burlap like a snug fitting bonnet and a shovel lay across it. Les passed around the edge of the crowd and then stood next to Principle Wayne.

A white van honked as it drove by on Mill River Road and some in the crowd turned to see who the rude invader of their quiet moment could be. Les scanned the gathering and was surrounded by many people he had never seen before, but in the second row his friend P.J. Woods stood in solemn reverence. The blue lenses of his sunglasses twinkled in the light as P.J. gave a quick nod of recognition that tossed a squiggle of blond locks down across his forehead.

Les waited for everyone to turn back around and was annoyed that he didn't see Eddie's face staring at him. She never broke a promise even when it meant missing a classic car show because she told her friend Bethany that she'd help her move that day. Les figured that things had changed a lot for her lately so he took a deep breath and let the anger fall away. He cleared his throat and unfolded the speech written in pencil.

"Thank you Principle Wayne. Aki, or as some of you know him Akihide, was my friend. I can't believe it's been six months since he passed. The accident seems like yesterday. Aki was a talented artist who taught me how to draw and introduced me to a whole new world. As some of you know, he and I were into comics. We both got into them as kids but I didn't read them as much as I got older.

That changed when I broke my leg and was stuck inside for months. Aki came over and shared new books with me until one day I showed him my sketches. He told me if I practiced I could probably draw pretty well someday. He started to teach me and then took me to my first con, sorry, comic book convention. From then on, we wrote and drew stories together. They weren't that good at first but we got better with practice. Together, we create numerous characters and stories. I owe him for helping me, teaching me, and encouraging me. He never wanted anything in return.

Aki never hurt anyone. He never lied even if he probably should have. He shared everything with everyone like you were a part of his family and helped you when you needed it," Les said but had to stop to clear his throat and take a slow breath to stop from tearing up.

He continued, "Sorry. Aki was a great artist even at seventeen. He could do black and white portraits as real as a photo and paint landscapes like I had never seen before. One day, I hope I can be even half as good. He was also one of the smartest people I ever met but never showed off and made you feel smarter by being around him. He was one of the best people I ever met and made me better by being my friend. I don't know what I'm going to do without him. I miss him more than I thought I could and always will."

Gentle sobs escaped from the crowd and tears blinked out of Les's eyes as he wiped them dry. He folded the speech and bowed. Principle Wayne put his hand on Les's shoulder.

"Good job Lester. And now we will plant this dogwood in honor of Akihide Kubo," Principle Wayne said.

The town's head landscaper, Mr. Banner, walked over in dusty green overalls. He knelt down and a razor knife flashed as it sliced the burlap. Principle Wayne handed Les the shovel and helped Mr. Banner tug off the covering. They placed the root ball into the hole and Les tossed in the damp dirt and packed it tight.

The ceremony was done and the crowd began to disperse. Les looked over to P.J. and gave him a nod. P.J. lifted his iPhone, pointed at it twice, and waved once. Les nodded and knew to call him later. P.J. drifted away with the crowd and Les wondered where Eddie could be. It wasn't like her to miss something so important.

Mr. and Mrs. Logan, arm in arm, walked their son back to the car.

A mile from home, Mrs. Logan turned around in the passenger seat and looked at Les playing a game on his phone.

"It was nice of Principle Wayne to head the memorial considering school is out," she said.

"Yeah. Hey Mom, could you let Wooly out when we get home? I want to get out of these clothes," Les asked.

"Sure, but you have to feed him. Speaking of food, are you going to eat breakfast with us Hamster?" Mrs. Logan asked.

"Maybe, but I'm going to work on the comic first," Les said.

"Fine, but there are things we need to talk about today. Okay?" Mr. Logan asked.

"Okay."

It was a clear morning, warm and bright, but a strange chill came over Les as they passed by Upton College.

Chapter 3: Phantom dial

On a quaint side street named Lynbrook Lane, the Logan family's yellow house with black shutters sat under the partial shade of a massive oak tree. Mr. Logan's Nissan sedan parked in the driveway and the family got out one at a time. The rooster weathervane on top of the garage spun in the growing breeze as yips, barks, and howls could be heard coming from inside the house. Mr. Logan unlatched the front door and Mrs. Logan distracted their Labradoodle while Les went straight upstairs.

In his room, a room with two closets and two windows, Les sat at his cluttered desk and stared at the computer monitor. The unfinished mini-comic that Aki and he started on Halloween about an abandoned alien who ate human hair glowed on the screen. With light pressure, his sensor tip pen swept across the touch screen display of his drawing tablet that was tilted up forty-five degrees next to his keyboard. He stopped drawing and examined the black and white panels of the digital comic on the monitor. His frustration was building up like the heat in his room that was seeping in through the cracked window. The hot air was making the scattered piles of laundry on the floor cast off the scents of fabric softener, dog, and stinky socks.

"Why can't I do this?" Les asked himself.

He wiped a bead of sweat from his forehead and sat back in his office chair his mother bought at a tag sale. Les placed the pen down, closed his eyes, and balled up his fists. A deep breath couldn't stop the surging anger and he slammed his fists on the surface of the desk.

"I know why, I suck," Les said.

He opened his eyes and unclenched his fists. The computer monitor flickered as Les shook his head.

"Can't do this without him. Might as well bail."

Les spun around in his chair and looked to the wall where a framed sketch from his favorite artist Skottie Young hung next to the light switch. In the corner where the wall and ceiling met, gray wisps of cobwebs fluttered in the rising warm air.

"No more," Les said, spun back around and exited the files.

With a few clicks of the mouse, he went online to check his emails and see if anything interesting was happening on Youbentmywookie.com. Nothing was new in the world of comics or SciFi so he went on Facebook and updated his status to BORED. The bark of his dog Wooly Bully skimmed up through the second story window.

"The alarm calls," he said.

Les pushed back against the desk to get up and accidentally jammed the desk into the wall. The nine inch model of a Gundam robot on the corner teetered and fell. It crashed on an open patch of hardwood floor. The red and blue enamel paint on the broken pieces of plastic glittered in the light falling through his pane glass window.

"Damn it Bob. Not you too. Aki would be screaming if he saw you like this. I'll deal with you later," he said.

At the sill, Les ratcheted the window open, popped his head out and scanned the backyard. A halo of sunlight crowned his neighbor's tar shingle roof across the way. He looked down to the backyard enclosed by a simple split rail fence weathered gray with time.

"Quiet Wooly. Food's coming," he said.

Les zipped down the side staircase and through the kitchen to the back door. The dog, all wagging tail and white curls, trotted inside with high steps. He headed right for his metal bowl sitting below the island countertop where the cobalt blue tiles bounced a cool light across the kitchen. Les grabbed the bag of dog food from the pantry. The scent of hour old bacon hung near the stove.

The dry food rang in the bowl and before Les could finish pouring Wooly Bully began to munch it down. Ten gulps were all it took the dog to make the dish shine as bright as his white teeth.

"Could you come to the table Les, your father and I want to talk to you," his mother said from around the corner.

"Sure Mom," he said and put the dog food back in the pantry.

Les grabbed a bottle of pomegranate flavored water from the fridge and walked into the breakfast nook where his parents were seated. Wooly Bully followed close behind and went under the round glass-top table. Les sat down across from his father and watched him push his laptop to the side after making sure the power cable was plugged into the wall.

Mr. Logan sat back in his padded chair and straightened the collar of his wrinkled shirt. Mrs. Logan stood and picked up a bowl of fruit. She offered it to Les but he waved his hand no so she went in the kitchen.

"So?" Les asked.

"When are you going to clean up the pig pen you got up there?" Mr. Logan asked.

"Not this again. You said my room was my room and I could have it anyway I wanted if I got good grades. I did," Les said.

"I was talking about painting the walls or moving the bed. What if company comes over?" Mr. Logan asked.

"We have company like twice a year, Christmas and Thanksgiving. What's this really about?" Les asked.

Mr. Logan rubbed his hard cornered chin.

"It's about what you want," Mr. Logan said.

Mrs. Logan stood framed in the doorway. She put her glasses on and walked back to the table.

"Actually, it's more about your plans. We talked about you getting a job since the economy has been rough for me and your father," Mrs. Logan said.

She flattened her white skirt behind her knees and sat.

"I know but school just ended," Les said.

"All the more reason to get out there. This town doesn't have many businesses that are hiring so you have to jump on it now," Mr. Logan said.

"Like anyone would hire me," Les said.

Mr. Logan took a deep breath into his barrel chest and exhaled with a whistle.

"I just got the job at Solarian, and the economy is shaky, so if you want to get that digital Cynic thing you talked about, you'll have to buy it yourself," Mr. Logan said and Les rubbed his forehead in hard circles.

"It's Cintiq dad. It's for drawing," Les said.

"Fine, but if you want to get that or go anywhere like the comic book convention, you'll have to pay for it," Mr. Logan said.

"Not going," Les said.

"Why not? You've been talking about it for a year," Mrs. Logan asked.

At that moment, the laptop's screen went black. Mr. Logan and Les both noticed. After a fizzling sound came from the wall, the screen came alive with power.

"That's odd. Must be a power surge from everyone having their AC's on full blast," Mr. Logan said.

"Remember to back everything up Dad. Don't want to have that problem like you did with the last machine," Les said.

His father nodded and unplugged the laptop's power cable from the wall outlet.

"So why aren't you going?" Mrs. Logan asked.

"My work isn't good enough. I can't do it without him," Les said.

Mr. Logan's face softened with a deep frown.

"You've been through enough today Les. Why don't you just relax and look for a job online tomorrow," Mr. Logan said.

"Remember Les, Aki isn't really gone and will always be with you," Mrs. Logan said.

"He's dead Mom," Les said and his chair grated on the floor as he pushed it back.

He left his parents in silence as Wooly Bully followed him up to his room and planted down on the tallest pile of laundry on the floor. Les closed the door and grabbed his cell phone from the nightstand. He had a text from Eddie.

L, so sorry. Mom N Dad @ war. Will water the tree L8R. Sorry. E
That makes sense Les thought.

"Sucks for Eddie. I think she wants out of here more than I do," Les said to Wooly Bully who looked up and tilted his furry head.

At his computer, Les went online and signed into World of Warcraft as a cool draft entered under the door and swirled across the floor. Loose papers and protein bar wrappers fluttered beneath the bed as the chill raced over the dog. Wooly Bully's ears flattened and his tail lowered as he skittered over to the desk chair. Not looking, Les swung his arm back and pet the dog.

"What's up?"

The dog backed away and a cold patch of air fell across Les's legs exposed below his khaki shorts.

"Mom turned on the AC? No way. Better go ask or they'll blame me Wooly," Les said and headed to the door.

He opened the door and the heat of the hall draped over him.

"Hey Mom! You turn on the AC? Should I shut my windows?" he asked.

The sounds of chairs being pushed back from the breakfast table rolled up the stairs.

"The AC isn't on Les. You know we don't put it on until it gets over ninety," Mrs. Logan said.

"Okay," Les said, closed the door and continued, "more like a hundred. Don't know how old people sleep in the heat."

At his computer, Les started to play World of Warcraft but wasn't in the mood so he signed off and went into Facebook. He scrolled through new photos, comments, videos, and wondered if people realized that all the stuff they post never goes away. On his nightstand, his old flip phone vibrated.

"Not now."

He swiped the phone, flipped it open, but lost his grip when he saw a phone number that shouldn't be calling. The phone dropped onto his pillow.

"No way. That didn't just happen."

The phone kept vibrating as Les took a deep breath and thought okay pick it up. Your eyes are just playing tricks.

The phone stopped buzzing. Les's hand shook as he scooped it up. His eyes didn't deceive him and a voice-mail was left.

"Crazy. Has to be a glitch in the phone network. That's all."

Les sat on the edge of his bed. The mattress coils squeaked and groaned as he shifted his weight. Wooly Bully walked over and sat at Les's feet. The dog looked over his shoulder at Les with bright amber eyes. Les pet the dog's head and opened the voice mail that came from Aki's old cell number. He heard static but then a faint voice said "Rachel" and then the message ended. He clapped the phone shut and dropped it.

"Phone's gotta be messed up. Seriously losing it. So need to get out of here. Hey Wooly, how about we go skating in a minute? Outside Wooly. Outside," Les said.

He swung the door open and the dog trotted out with his tail wagging in circles. Wooly Bully's toenails clicked and clacked on the hardwood floor as he walked down the hallway. Les updated his Facebook status to read: FREAKED OUT. 100 IN MY ROOM BUT GOT A CHILL. THEN SOMEHOW AKI'S CELL # CALLED. CAN'T BELIEVE IT'S BEEN 6 MONTHS. BTW, NEED A JOB.

P.J. posted a comment on Les's status a few seconds later: Miss him 2 L. Still hear his voice but don't get calls. Could be a prank.

Les thought P.J. was right and someone was probably playing a cruel joke but he had no idea who it could be. He figured maybe someone posted a comment on Aki's Facebook page that would give him a clue so he decided to check it out. Les hadn't been able to look at the comments on Aki's page since he died but mustered up the courage and went to the profile that had since been transformed into a digital memorial. His eyes got cloudy as he reads comments about Aki's art.

"People should tell people stuff when they're alive," Les said, logged out and dug out his skateboard from under his laundry on the floor.

The broken model sitting on the floor grabbed Les's attention so he picked up the colorful plastic pieces of the Gundam robot and put them on the desk next to the black jewelry box that held his grandfather's watch that the cops found at the accident. His mother had it fixed months ago but Les never opened the box.

"All shiny and broken," Les said and shook his head.

Outside on the front yard, Wooly Bully was hitched to a blue leash and Les placed headphones snug on his mop top. The skateboard dropped to the cement sidewalk and the hard wheels clacked with the impact. Les hopped on goofy-footed and Wooly Bully took off like a draft horse pulling Les down the even streets of New Hebron. They headed towards downtown where the train station cut the suburb in two. One side was for locals and the other was for Upton College. Skating normally cleared Les's head but all he could think about was the creepy voice-mail.

Chapter 4: Tuition

New Hebron was a suburb fifty miles from New York City with streets and lanes lined with pine and sycamore. Like most suburbs, it hid problems and one section of town was practically owned by Upton College. Their esteemed psychology department had a professor named Harold Gluck who was doing unsanctioned research from his house on Brookside Lane just a few streets down from campus. The school gave him slack because he won a grant years ago that looked good on the school's sales pitch to parents, but there was a limit and he was about to cross it.

In a white lab coat, Professor Gluck stood behind his research assistant Lazlo who sat hunched over a keyboard with his face to a computer monitor. The array of computers hummed in the second floor study. They went through data that the internet spiders and data bots collected while the scent of bleach wafted in from the bathroom down the hall. The information they collected brought back a possible target. They had been watching the target for months because his closest friend Akihide Kubo died in a car accident six month earlier.

"I knew if we watched the friends and family of a teenager who recently deceased it would pay off with a possible personal haunting. And now, here we are coming back to Mr. Les Logan," Professor Gluck said and brushed the sweat from his high forehead.

"It seems you were right Professor. The spectral units localize around known areas. What now?" Lazlo asked.

"We should go through his online history. Dig into his public information to see if he has been contacted before," Professor Gluck said.

"I already know his history. You had me go through it when he posted that his friend died," Lazlo said.

"You remember it all?"

"That's why you hired me."

"Of course, of course, guess I am a scatter brain like Dr. Julius says. Would you like some water?" Professor Gluck asked.

Lazlo nodded his head, tufts of copper hair bounced down across his face, and Professor Gluck made his way to a side table by the bay window. A bronze pitcher reflected the day through the converted bedroom as he poured two glasses of water. Professor

Gluck passed Lazlo a tall glass. The rims of the glasses dinged together.

"Cheers," Professor Gluck said.

"Cheers," Lazlo said and sniffed the water, "lemon?"

"Why yes, lemon actually reduces fatigue and I can't have you getting sleepy on me. So, refresh my scattered brain on Lester Logan," Professor Gluck said.

Lazlo's fingers flew across the keyboard and brought up Les Logan's profile.

"Les is seventeen and from what I could tell played hockey until he was a freshman at New Hebron High. Broke his leg, started drawing and met Akihide Kubo who was, as Les called him, 'the best artist in the P.O.S town'" Lazlo said as Professor Gluck waved his hand.

"What's P.O.S?"

"Uh, not good Professor. It's just an acronym for crappy."

"Oh. Please forgive my old man ignorance."

"You're only in your forties."

"True, I just didn't want to let on that my knowledge of popular culture was so limited. Being out of touch is a disadvantage."

"And now back to Lester. His father was an engineer and now works in renewable energy at Solarian. His mother works at a tea distributor and she practices aroma therapy, or 'the stinky' as Les calls it. So she is probably a New Age type, which could be helpful. Looks like Les took his friends death pretty hard and though many people posted condolences on his Facebook profile he only responds to two friends, a P.J Woods and an Eddie Nash. His interests include art and at one time posted that he was planning to go to the big ComicCon in New York with Akihide this fall. Otherwise he listens to a wide variety of music, skates, and does generally dull teenage things. No evidence of drug slang, gang affiliation, ADHD, mental illness and no interest in the occult. And now, he's looking for a job. On a side note about Akihide Kubo, I found that he was an organ donor if that has any bearing."

"Not that I can think of. Are there gangs around here Lazlo?" Professor Gluck asked.

"You'd be surprised Professor but no. New Hebron is safe. Just pretend gangs," Lazlo said.

"Okay, keep an eye on him. Monitor all of his activities for any spectral unit contact or infiltration. Hopefully we can lure the spirit consciousness to the containment cell through Les."

...

Down the even streets on the other side of town, Les and Wooly Bully zipped by P.J.'s house over the new pavement, soft and smelling of tar. His only thought was on what was in front of him. The dog ran close to the sidewalk and bass beats filtered out of Les's headphones into the airspace surrounding his head.

A squirrel, alerted to Wooly Bully in full gallop, scurried up a tree to escape and triggered the dog's chase instinct. The slack of the leash went tight when Wooly Bully surged and almost dragged Les off the skateboard but with a hard kick he regained his balance. Then, a tan Jeep Wrangler rumbled up beside Les. He looked up to see P.J. Woods with his oversized blue sunglass staring at him.

P.J. pointed to the expansive gray house with the wrap around deck coming up and Les nodded. The Jeep pulled out in front, sped up, and took the hard corner into the driveway that sent a screech through the prim neighborhood. The Jeep came to a heavy halt. Wooly Bully wasn't bothered in the least by the harsh sound and kept trotting towards the house he had visited many times before.

They came to a stop at the driveway. Les took off his headphones and hooked them around his neck as he looked at the grand home. The house always reminded Les of a plantation in old Civil War movies. P.J., hands in his short's pockets, walked out to the street. A UPS truck roared down the road, hopping up and down over a couple potholes, and left thick diesel exhaust behind.

"Fumes. Gross. Hey P.J., shouldn't you be at Jujitsu?" Les asked.

"Not today. Went looking for you because you didn't call or answer your cell. Your mother said you were went skating like two hours ago," P.J. said.

"Stopped at the park to get Wooly some water. Wow, has it been that long? Shit," Les said.

"Dude, you're gonna have to watch your language around me. I made a bet with my father and if I don't swear for the summer, boom, backpacking across Europe with a Eurail pass. So please, be careful, I don't want to accidentally slip," P.J. said and the two bumped fists.

"Funny, you swear more than anyone. Good luck with that," Les said.

"Thanks, where's your ancient device?"

"Left the phone home alone," Les said.

"You're the only person I know who'll go out without their device," P.J. said.

"Not really a device, it's just a crappy phone."

"Come on, let's go sit on the porch," P.J. said.

Les nodded and they walked across the wide lawn scored with diagonal lines from the recent mow. Up on the front porch, where a white washed banister ran atop spindle supports, they sat on matching wicker chairs. P.J.'s mother pulled the shade back from inside and peeped out. When she recognized who was sitting on the porch, she waved from behind the window. Les waved back. Wooly Bully collapsed in a heap between P.J and Les. The dog's tongue dripped down to the deck.

"Prepare for lemonade," P.J. said.

"Nice, I'm fu… sorry, really dry," Les said.

"So bro, Aki's number rang you?"

"Yeah, it was weird. A message was left too. Wasn't clear but I heard something. Don't know man? Brain is mush and I haven't drawn anything good in weeks."

"Was it Aki's voice? What'd the message say?" P.J. asked.

"It was fuzzy. Don't think it was an old message from him either. It just said Rachel. Don't know any Rachels," Les said.

"Me neither. That's whacked man. Probably just some fool jerking you around so put it out ya mind. Hey, you still working on that comic you and Aki were putting together?"

"Was, sort of stopped. Wasn't getting anywhere with it and was stressing."

"Anything else stressing you out?"

"Getting ready to send my stuff into SVA."

"NYC right?"

"Yup, New York School of Visual Arts. We were both going to apply."

"Didn't know that. But hey, you want to know about stress, I asked Martin out," P.J. said.

"The exchange student from Argentina?" Les asked.

"The very one."

"Didn't think he was gay but good for you man," Les said and shut his mouth as he heard a lock tumble in the front door.

Mrs. Woods bumped the front door open with her rear end that was draped in a tennis skirt and she exited with a silver platter. The ice in the glasses rattled while she walked over and set a tray down on a glass table next to the railing.

"Hello Les," she said.

"Hello Mrs. Woods. How are you today?" Les asked.

"I'm wonderful and it's so nice of someone to ask," she said.

"Mom quit the drama. I talked to you like two hours ago. Little late for tennis don't you think?" P.J. asked.

"I'm meeting your father at the club for dinner and the girls are there so I decided to join them for the day," she said.

"So dinner is…?" P.J. asked.

"A dial away," she said.

P.J. leaned back in his chair and rolled his eyes back.

"Of course. Tah mother. And thanks for the drinks," P.J. said.

"You're welcome. Lock up when you leave and remember your curfew is midnight. Buh bye Les," she said and spun away.

P.J. got up and poured. They waited with closed lips until the garage door buzzed open around the corner of the house and Les looks up to P.J.

"They know right?" Les asked.

"I thought I told you like a year ago. They've known since we watched Attack of the Sith in the new home theatre and I said Anakin was hot."

"Oh yeah. Sorry. Like I said, been mushy lately. You know I worry about you. People are fu… sorry, really stupid out there and you need to be careful who you tell," Les said.

"That's why I love you dude, and you know what I mean. You're a strong dude, and I heard what you did to the Goon, but you shouldn't worry about me. Me. A trained MMA fighter with black belts in Jeet Kun Do and Brazilian Jujitsu. And no losses I might add."

"That's kind of what I'm getting at. What if those dudes find out?"

"What? They're going to attack me. They already do. Plus, if they attack because they're all freaked out, it makes them easier to beat down. No fear kid. Can't live in fear."

"Sometimes it feels like that's all I have," Les said.

They both waved as Mrs. Woods drove away in her dark green Range Rover and then P.J. sat back.

"Dude, you have me. You have Eddie. You have your art. That's more than a lot of people. Speaking of Eddie, is she driving tonight?"

"Damn, spaced on that. I think so. She didn't say anything about not going out when she texted me. Uh, could you give me and Wooly a lift home? I need to get some things done before we head out," Les said.

"Sure."

After drinks, the house security system was set. Les and Wooly followed P.J. to his Jeep and as P.J. slipped in the driver's seat, Wooly Bully leapt into the back with his tongue still dragging. Slobber dripped until the dog shook his head. Drool splattered across the dashboard and windshield.

"You're cleaning the dog spit off the dash," P.J. said.

"Dude, that's nothing. By the time we get to my house, your backseat is going to be drenched. Gonna need towels."

"What a time to leave the handi-wipes in my gym bag."

The engine chugged as they drove down the even streets. The sound of lawnmowers and leaf blowers churned between the houses as the suburban incense of grilled burgers and hotdogs begun to saturate the early afternoon from lunchtime cook outs. All seemed serene in New Hebron, but underneath the calm, things were changing. Plots were being formed.

Chapter 5: Summer time rolls.

An amber twilight came on the edge of the day and Les waited out on the stoop for Eddie and P.J. to pick him up. Dinner with his parents was short, silent, and he noticed the quick glances his parents stole but didn't quite know what to make of it. A blue behemoth, a spot of ocean on the land, rolled around the corner and caught Les's eye. Eddie's prized nineteen sixty-seven Pontiac Bonneville convertible, creamy smooth, came to a stop on the curb in front of Les. Wooly Bully barked from the window and Les waved to the dog. Wooly Bully stopped and disappeared.

At the helm, almost consumed by the size of the car, Eddie with her Coca Cola eyes was draped in fifties vintage clothes. She tapped the steering wheel like a bongo as her horn rimmed glasses perched at the tip of her nose. When Les looked at Eddie, he was reminded of a photo of his grandmother May when she was not much older than him at a Buddy Holly concert. His grandmother told him she went to the concert and it changed her life. Taught her she could do things on her own.

"Stop standing there kid. Destiny awaits," P.J. said from the passenger seat.

"Oh, my bad," Les said and tumbled over the back quarter panel of the car and into the deep backseat.

Flat on his back, Les looked over the tan upholstered seats to see Eddie and P.J. with raised eyebrows staring back.

"If you scratched Biggie Blue, I'll take you to Michael Jackson's doctor for a visit," Eddie said.

"Don't worry, I slid. No scuff," Les said.

He was pinned to the seat when Eddie jammed on the gas pedal.

Flat on his back, Les stared at his beat up Nikes that rested on the car's frame behind the passenger seat. He thought the shoes won't last him through the summer.

"L, your feet stink," P.J. said.

"Not as much as your cologne bro," Les said.

P.J. turned around and looked at Les. He pulled the collar of his white tuxedo shirt to his nose and sniffed.

"You're joking, right?" P.J. asked.

"Sensitive much? Calm down. Just a joke, I'm sure Martin will be all a flutter," Les said.

A smack from the driver's side flew to P.J.'s shoulder.

"Dick, you didn't tell me about Martin," Eddie said.

"I was going to show you. It's a much more effective way of surprising you, but now you know," P.J. said.

"Put on some tunes please, I know you got satellite radio on this cabin cruiser like a month ago," Les said.

"I have the gear but, uh, signing up is another thing. Gotta pay for it myself. Speaking of that. Saw you need a job too. If you want we can look together on Monday," Eddie asked.

"Cool," Les said.

A new iPhone slipped out of P.J.'s pocket. He held it up to the fading light of the day.

"We can't cruise in silence. I have Pandora on my phone. It's free. Have a cable?" P.J. asked.

Eddie pointed to the glove box where he found all that he needed and hooked his phone into Biggie Blue. He flicked and scrolled the touch screen. A final decisive hit of the fingertip activated the App. P.J. rolled his neck so that he could look right at Eddie whose face was streaked in street light.

"In my research into ancient music, I came across this guy Jeff Buckley from the nineties. He drowned in a river in Memphis when he was like thirty. Holy pipes on this guy. You'll love it Eddie," P.J. said.

He looked over the back seat and down to Les.

"You maybe not so much," P.J. said and Les shrugged.

P.J. turned back around and chewed this thumb nail while he leaned back. The song "Last Good Bye' came on and embraced the evening flowing over the convertible.

The half-moon hung high in the half-night and made Les wonder if Luna was going to be at the party. The thought of her made his chest tight and his ears hot. He just couldn't control himself around her.

The three friends looked through the crushed orange light of sunset falling across their town with eyes that only seventeen year olds have. Soon, they traversed the town they knew so well and ended up parking at the end of a cul-de-sac where a golf course was fenced off through a line of pine trees. The street was cluttered with kids texting and cars parked half on the grass.

The graduation party their friend Hector was throwing at his parent's house, or as Hector called it the Big McMansion, was under way. Bass beats boomed from music coming from the backyard that was as long the first hole of the golf course. An airplane flew low over head sending down an expanding wail of engine noise over the ruckus of the party and then trailed off in slow degrees as it flew towards the Westchester airport.

P.J., with Eddie and Les following behind, navigated the crowd standing outside the front porch. Nods of recognition bounced through the music. The three made their way through the house jammed wall to wall and passed by the living room where Hector's brother Emile sat with his college friends, all with backward caps, playing Madden Football on X-box.

Through the sliding glass door to the backyard patio, the three saw just how serious the party was. Clusters of cliques took up the yard just outside of where the deck lights couldn't reach. Everyone held a red plastic cup or a phone in hand. Some held both.

"This is like Rock Star man," P.J. said and led out onto the patio.

The floodlights momentarily snatched their sight as they slipped into the shade of the yard. The three stopped, huddled up and then looked around for familiar faces.

"Going to roam kids. Mostly seniors here but I snagged a look at Luna over by the fence there L. Eddie you want to come with?" P.J. asked.

"No, go. I'm taking L over to Luna," Eddie said.

"Right on. Text me if you need me," P.J. said.

"I don't have my phone," Les said.

"What are you a leper? Dude, how do you…? Never mind, I won't leave without telling you. Go. Hit on the girl you've sulked after since fifth grade," P.J. said and revolved out into the dark crowd.

"Come on L, I can feel things are going to happen for you," Eddie said.

"Another one of your psychic visions?" Les asked.

"Yeah and don't make fun of me. You know my gift is real," Eddie said.

"Never said it wasn't," Les said.

"Let's go," Eddie said and grabbed Les by the arm.

The scent of fresh water from the golf course's nearby water hazard drifted on the breeze that spiraled through the backyard party. Les looked down at the ground as Eddie tugged him along over to the fence where Luna Lowery and Arden Lane, friends since birth, stood and sipped from red cups. Eddie let go of his arm and waved to the girls. The girls waved back but Arden looked away from Les. Her hair fell across her hazel eyes as a black veil.

"Hey girls, what's the sitch?" Eddie asked.

"No parents, obv. There's a keg back there and this place is soaked with college guys," Luna said and tossed back her blond locks.

"Meat heads or like cool?" Eddie asked.

"Cool, mostly. Half of the party left to go to Tower's though. Hi Les," Luna said.

"Hey Luna, Arden, how's it?" Les asked.

"Good, oh, my father wanted me ask you if your dad wanted to sell that convertible Fiat?" Luna asked.

"Nah, my dad loves that thing," Les replied.

"Arden loves that car, don't you?" Luna asked.

"Yeah, it shines," Arden said.

"Why don't you take her for a ride sometime Les," Luna asked.

"I don't drive since…," Les said just as Emile, bound in his college lacrosse jersey, barreled through the crowd and barged over to the fence.

"Hey Luna, long time," Emile said.

"Hi Emile, yeah it's been a crazy long time, like a year. How'd you like college," Luna said.

Emile puffed up.

"It's great. Nothing like high school. You're going to be a senior next year right?" Emile asked her. Eddie and Les looked at each other

"Yeah," Luna said.

"Cool. Come inside. Leave the losers to the mosquitoes. Bring your friend," Emile said and turned away.

He turned back halfway and beckoned them with a wave.

"Okay," Luna said, grabbed Arden's arm and they walked off.

Arden waved to Les as she stepped into the light coming from the deck.

"He didn't even say hello," Les said.

"I know. What a tool," Eddie said.

"Let's go to Tower's," Les said.

"Yeah. I don't know if I can tolerate Emile and friends. Let's find P.J."

They waded through the swirling crowds, smacked mosquitoes away, and came upon P.J. surrounded by a group of sophomore girls in pastel sundresses. They explained the situation to him as the girls looked on with amorous intent not knowing their gaze will never be returned. Through the protests of P.J.'s adoring audience, Eddie grabbed his sleeve and began to pull him away.

"You all have my digits, going to Tower's," P.J. said to the group.

As the three walked around the side of the house, Les stopped.

"Why do girls always go with older guys even if they're jerks?" he asked.

"It's genetic kid," P.J. said.

"Sometimes people see what they want and are blind to the sketchy stuff," Eddie said.

They got to the car, hopped in, and pulled out right as two cop cars, lights off, parked on the cul-de-sac.

"Fail," P.J. said.

"True," Les said.

Off to the Tower's they drove covered by a sheet of warm night. They passed through the downtown and train station as they finally breached outskirts of town. Private roads were dotted with post mailboxes that indicated the hidden estates and soon they reached Weston Park where the rural streets were as dark as wet ink and the starry sky above poked through the canopy of night with pricks of distant light. They pulled onto an access road camouflaged by hedges, a secret to teenagers and park workers alike. Dry gravel crunched under the tires as they parked by a broken rail fence.

"Hope they're here," P.J. said and popped the car door open.

"Nice. Haven't been to Gumby Land for a long time," Les said.

"Why in the hell do they call it that?" Eddie asked.

"Don't really know. It's what people have been calling this place for years but I think there was a family of deformed people that had heads that looked like Gumby and the government stole their land and put them in institutions," Les said.

"Saw an episode of Gumby on Hulu. Boring. Wait. Hold on. My phone is buzzing," P.J. said. He pulled out his phone from his stone gray shorts and read the screen.

"Martin's up there," P.J. said.

Their eyes adjusted to the evening as they went up the trail towards the hills. The walk got harder as the ground steepened until they broke through a tree line and made their way out to a manmade clearing. A huge cut in the forest extended in both directions for miles and in the middle a line of metal-boned relay towers were connected like ski lifts along a series of rolling hills that sent electricity to New Hebron. They made their way by couples making out underneath chestnut trees and down to the rock outcropping that formed a natural amphitheatre below the nearest tower. The locals called it Tower's Rock. Four fires burned in rusted oil drums that cast a diffuse orange light into the night at each corner of the outcropping where the chatter of teenagers slipped away.

Through the flickering light, P.J. spotted Martin down below as he sipped a beer. His linen shirt fluttered in the heat rolling off the fire.

"Dudes, I'm going over by the ledge. Have fun mingling," P.J. said and sifted through the outlines of people surrounding the fires.

Eddie shrugged. Les shrugged.

"So down in the Dip or over by the stairs?" Les asked.

"Wanted to go over to the ledge since it has the best view, but let's go to the stairs," Eddie said.

Down the sloping path, worn by thousands of teenage soles, they made their way to a group of terraced stones that jutted out to create a natural patio. The chirps of crickets called out from the brush and mixed with the eager chatter of teenagers to create an unending noise that blanketed the area. The three friends were greeted by nods, hellos, and quick waves as they approached.

"Yo, Eddie. Over here," Eddie's friend Bethany said from down in a section called the Dip, a rock formation that looked like a spoon.

"Hey Bettie Pin-Up, I'll be there in a sec. Is it…?" she asked.

"Go," Les said and sat on a flat stone just outside the grasp of the oil drum's light.

As Eddie left, a group of three led by a lanky guy named Dan strolled up wearing t-shirts too tight for their chests. The jumpy steps of their stylized walks bounced the gold chains dangling outside their shirts.

"Hey hey L," Dan said.

"That you Dan?" Les asked.

"Yup it's Danny Boy yo," he said.

"How's it?" Les asked.

"Profits are soaring and bitches are moaning," Dan said.

"Oh, okay," Les said.

"Ize gots the pill to chillz your illz," Dan said and the others sat down besides Les.

"Hey Barry, George," Les said.

They nodded and crossed their tan, bony teenage arms.

"So, you in need?" Dan said.

"No, not like I have any money anyway," Les said.

"That's cool. Here, have a Xanax, nobody wants theses. Everyone wants Dr. House to make a call and Addi," Dan said and passed him a pill.

"Thanks," Les replied, took the pill, and said, "In a bit. Night's early."

"True. They're good though. Took one bout two hours ago. Sip some hooch and things get gooey ya know?" Dan said.

"You guys know if anyone's hiring in town?" Les asked.

"Nah, no one. Why'd ya think we dish the scripts?" Barry said.

"Sucks," Les said.

"Yup. Hey man just wanted to say what happened was crazy," Dan said.

"Yeah, it was," Les said.

"Aki was good people. Did that crazy ass logo for me when I was trying to DJ," George said.

"That was pretty hype," Barry said.

"You draw too right?" Dan asked.

"Sort of but…"

"Sort of what?" Barry asked.

"Don't know, don't have the skills Aki had. Don't know if I can even draw anymore. Hands are still shaky sometimes."

"Sucks, well, if you ever want to come with the crew and roll this summer we park at the Nike site," Dan said.

Les scratched his knee and then looked up at Dan.

"I don't drive anymore man," Les said.

"Oh wellz. Later L," Dan said.

Barry and George got up and they slipped into the crowd by the fires. Les didn't think one Xanax could hurt, it was a weak prescription after all, and it might just take away the nerves that started to churn in his stomach. He looked at the pill and popped it.

After a few moments of nothing happening, Les stood up, put his hand in his pockets and walked up to the base of the metal tower. The sign reading "Danger High Voltage" hung on a rusted bolt over Les's head. He looked up and imagined the electricity streaming through the wires like kids on a waterslide. Then everything stopped.

Xanax calmed most people's anxiety but for Les, it left gaps in time. The next thing he knew, he was in the front seat of Eddie's car parked in front of his house. Les looked to the back seat and no one was there.

"Where's P.J.?" Les asked.

Eddie ratcheted her head over to look at him.

"Uh, he stayed and we left. Oh shit! You don't remember. I knew you were rolling but what the hell did you take?"

"Xanax."

"You know what that crap does to you. Remember what happened when you took those anti-depressants so you could come back to school?"

"Yeah, it was dumb."

"No wonder you climbed the tower. Dumb ass."

"I did what?"

Les straightened up and looked at Eddie with a face wrinkled up with embarrassment.

"You climbed to the first cross supports on the tower and just sat up there for like an hour."

"Really?"

"Really. So that talk about what we were going to do senior year is out the window," Eddie said.

"What did I say?"

"That you were going to hook up with Luna but I then convinced you that Arden was cooler, and I have to say cuter."

"Arden? She always looks away in disgust when I'm around."

"For an artist, you sure don't see thing too clearly. She turns away because she's nervous. You should definitely go for Arden."

"Don't know if I could make it mesh. What else did I say?"

"You were going to, hey there's your mom in the window," Eddie said.

There crouched down, chin to the sill, with the curtain swept back, Les's mother smiled. The front porch light flicked on.

"So?"

"You said you were going to do everything you could to get out of here."

"Thanks for everything Eddie. Got to bounce."

"Later L. You know where to find me if you need me. And be careful, I feel a strong presence around you. Don't know what, but I feel something."

"Thanks," Les said and stuck out his tongue.

"Cute," Eddie said.

Up in Les's room, Wooly Bully waited and jumped off the bed when the door creaked open. All Les heard as he entered was a clatter of toenails and all he could see was a blur of fur surging towards him.

"He was waiting for you," Les's mother said over the yips and squeals as the dog spun at Les's feet.

"He wasn't the only one," Les said and bent down to pet the dog and in moments was covered in dog slobber.

Wooly Bully watched Les wash his face in the shallow basin of the second floor bathroom and followed right behind as he went to his room. The dog hopped up on the bed and plopped down in the middle. Les turned on his computer and pulled up some old work.

On the screen, a page layout for a comic radiated in Les's eyes for what seemed like hours to him. A quick glance to the clock showed mere minutes had passed. In a daze, he went to the next page and set up a grid of four horizontal rectangles.

"What the hell am I doing? Screw it. Just going to work on that character sketch Wooly."

He clicked open another file and a digital page resolved with a black and white sketch of a slender teenage super hero. Half the character's body emitted a white aura and the other half was outlined by a thick darkness. The name above read Janus Chiaroscuro. The only name Aki and Les could agree on.

"So Wooly, Janus controls the light and the dark but not at the same time. Don't know what his weakness is yet, but every hero needs a weakness like every villain needs a strength. Let's see if I can copy this sketch Aki did."

The stylus was shaking in his hand as Les tried to draw but couldn't copy what was on the screen. He got the eyes right but not the proportions of the limbs. He deleted it and tried again, but this time drew the head too small. He deleted it. He tried again and again and again but never got it right. Les, fed up and glassy eyed, dropped the stylus pen down to his digital sketch pad.

"I'm no artist. Who am I kidding? I'm done. I quit Wooly. Good thing I can quit now and do something else with my life."

On his nightstand, his cell phone vibrated. It flipped and flopped like a fresh caught fish on the deck of a boat.

"Who the hell is calling me now?"

He took a deep breath and walked over. With a fast grab he opened the phone to see Aki's old number displayed.

"Messing with me huh? I'll play along and then."

He hits the call button.

"Okay jerk off. You better stop using this number to call me. It's not funny dick."

"It's me L. Aki."

The phone hit the floor. The battery popped out and slid under the bed. Les stared into space with his eyes as wide as his fear.

"That can't be. Sounds like him. Can't be him."

He knelt down to collect the battery and looked up to Wooly Bully. His ears were back on his shaggy white head.

As Les was about to put the battery in the phone, he saw a glow come from the face. It had power. Les's hand shook as he put the phone to his ear.

"Hello."

"Hey L. No time to explain now. Limited minutes. You need to help Rachel. I will call you when I figure this out. Later."

For a moment, Les forgot how to breathe, how to swallow and how to move. Wooly Bully shuffled over and nudged his hand with a cold nose. Les crashed down to the edge of the bed as the phone slipped from his hand and fell onto a pile of sweat stained t-shirts.

"I'm going nuts from that pill. That's it. Sleep time Wooly. I'll post it to see if anyone else is getting calls from Aki's old number just in case someone is being a punk."

So Les logged on and posted his problem to Facebook. He looked at the clock and rubbed his eyes as he crept back over to bed.

. . .

The next morning across town, Lazlo read Les's post and called Professor Gluck. The plan to study the phenomenon was set in motion.

Chapter 6: The offer.

Mrs. Logan piled fruit salad drizzled with lime juice on Les's plate next to his egg white and green pepper omelet as he rubbed the tired from his eyes. Mr. Logan closed his laptop and scooted it to the edge of the table as it charged.

"I wanted to say, I'm sorry for rushing you yesterday. Your mother and I discussed a few things last night while you were gone. Though I can't give you any money for art supplies, I will let you drive the Fiat. How about it?" Mr. Logan asked.

"Not going to buy any art supplies anyway and I don't want to drive right now. But thanks dad."

"How will you get to work?" Mrs. Logan asked.

"Any job in town is only like a mile away. I'll hoof it or skate."

"Well, if you want to make fifteen bucks, you can wash the Fiat," Mr. Logan said.

"All right. I'll do it in a few."

The serving fork clanged in the bowl of fruit salad as Mrs. Logan walked away from the table. She stopped at the doorway and faced Les.

"So what's this about not buying art supplies?" Mrs. Logan asked.

"Don't think it's the right path for me because I suck and all."

"You don't suck. You are very talented," Mrs. Logan said.

"No mom, Aki was talented."

"His father was an artist and Aki started much younger than you," Mr. Logan said.

"Do you think Aki would have wanted to make comics with you if he didn't think you were talented?" Mrs. Logan asked.

"My stories were better. His art was way better."

"So what if you get into SVA? What then?" Mr. Logan asked.

Les crouched over his plate and tapped a piece of cantaloupe with his fork. He dropped the fork and faced his father.

"I applied to other schools dad. Probably won't get into SVA anyway."

"I don't think you should quit drawing. You have talent and that's rare no matter what you hear. The only element missing is commitment," Mr. Logan said.

Mrs. Logan looked at her son with hopeful eyes.

"I don't know Dad. I'm going to check my messages and then I'll wash the car."

As Les climbed the stairs up to his room, Wooly Bully in tow, his parents sat next to each other in the breakfast nook. His father shook his head and his mother let out a deep sigh.

"Wish I could change him back to the way he was," Mrs. Logan said.

"What's done is done and he's going to have to find a way to move on," Mr. Logan said.

Up at his computer, Les saw that P.J. sent him a message. Wooly Bully hopped up on Les's bed, rubbed his nose on the sheet and stretched out. The hard scent of enamel paint scratched the inside of Les's nose as he sniffed the air. He opened a drawer in his desk to see that a vial of blue model paint had tipped over. The cap wasn't screwed on and half the contents had spilled out to glue pieces of paper and colored pencils together. He slid the drawer shut.

"How did that happen? Damn. I'll clean it later Wooly."

He read P.J.'s message and replied.

No. Didn't go crazy & yes. Made it home obv. & yes, got a phantom dial again but I was messed up. Ignore my post. Glad you had fun. Must wash a car. Later.

The garden hose coiled on the side of the house, caked with dirt, fought Les every inch out to the driveway where the Fiat, forest green and fast as its paint job, was parked. The tan convertible top was up.

The yellow sunlight poured down like thin ribbons of honey onto the hood. A black bucket filled with soap and water sloshed back and forth as Les hauled it out from the sink in the garage. He then grabbed a few sponges from the supply closet at the back of the tidy garage and walked out into the open day where the sky, brushed like blue oil paint across the horizon, was clear.

. . .

Across town, Professor Gluck read an email regarding his status from Dean Maecenus, the head of his department. He must publish or perish as his grants will not be renewed otherwise. A new smart phone dialed Lazlo's number. No answer. He waited to leave a voice mail.

"This is the Professor. I'm starting earlier than expected. I'm going over to meet this Lester Logan and begin the plan. I will talk to you in a few hours."

Professor Gluck looked up Lester Logan online. He found one listing for Logan in New Hebron at 515 Lynbrook Lane. Out in his Mini-Cooper, the professor tapped the address into his Garmin GPS. He drove towards Les's house with Guns N Roses cranked on the stereo and an arrow pointed the way on the GPS map.

At Les's house, the Fiat sparkled in the sun. The pollen of summer was now removed and water streaked down the sides of the car onto the smooth blacktop. Soapy rivulets ran into the street and cascaded into the storm drain. Les wiped the sweat from his face as his father poked his head out the front door and inspected the work.

"Looks good," Mr. Logan said and gave a quick nod.

Les nodded back with a half-grin.

At the corner of Lynbrook Lane and Lally Boulevard, Professor Gluck parked his car, took the Garmin GPS off his dashboard, and hid it under a lab coat in the front seat. He looked down the street and saw Les washing the Fiat.

"Perfect, has to be him," the professor said.

The Mini-Cooper was put in gear and drove down the street. Professor Gluck came to rest one house away from Les's groomed lawn. The door opened and Professor Gluck stepped out. He brushed back his thinning locks and pulled a piece of paper out of his shirt pocket. With short steps, he sauntered over to where the flow of soapy water ran into the storm drain and looks around as if confused.

"Hi there, could you tell me where Turkey Trot Lane is?" the professor asked. Les turned to look as his father came out the front door.

"Hello, looking for Turkey Trot?" Mr. Logan asked and patted his wrinkled shirt flat.

"Yes sir," Professor Gluck said.

"Well, hate to say but that's near the college on the other side of town," Mr. Logan said

"Really, must have taken a left when I should have taken a right after I got off the highway. I need to get one of those GPS devices," Professor Gluck said.

"Don't know how you ended up so far off course but what you have to do is go back out on Lally and then take a right, head about two miles straight through town and then when you come to Fox Run. Take a left and that will take you by the college and to Turkey Trot," Mr. Logan said.

"Thank you so much. I could have been wandering for days, but I guess that wouldn't be too bad. It's a lovely town. I'm renting a house on Brookside while I teach during the summer session at Upton," Professor Gluck said.

"Wonderful, welcome to New Hebron," Mr. Logan said.

"Thank you, your son?" Professor Gluck asked.

"Yes, he'll be a senior in high school next year," Mr. Logan said.

Looking back, Les twisted the sponge clean and rinsed it in the black bucket.

"You do good work," Professor Gluck said, looked right at Larry Logan and continued, "Your son wouldn't need a job would he? I need someone to do some gardening and also, I'm conducting a study that I need a couple teenagers for and he'd be paid well."

"You hear that Les?" Mr. Logan said.

"Yes."

"Sorry. How rude of me. My name is Harold Gluck, Dr. Harold Gluck but most just call me Professor Gluck," he said and stretched out his hand.

"Nice to meet you. Larry Logan, my son Les," Mr. Logan said and shook his hand.

"So Les, I'll pay you seventy-five dollars to come by once a week and do some yard work, but five hundred if you participate in my study. How about it?" Professor Gluck asked.

Les dropped the sponge and walked over to his father who crossed his arms.

"Sounds good, but what's the study?" Mr. Logan asked.

"It's a perception study that focuses on the development of the Pre-Frontal Cortex of the brain from puberty to adulthood. It's an examination into cognitive patterns and how young people process information through different regions of the brain at set times in their development. The range is fourteen to twenty-two and I need a seventeen year old," Professor Gluck said.

"How'd you know he was seventeen?" Mr. Logan asked.

With a quick turn of his head, Professor Gluck conjured up a sneeze, paused a moment and looked back.

"You said he was going to be a senior next year so I assumed…"

"Oh. Okay. Just let me verify you are working at the college and I'll let Les think about it. If wants to, he'll contact you. Sound fair?" Mr. Logan asked.

"Very. Can't be too careful these days. Here's my card," Professor Gluck said and slipped out a brown wallet bulging with premium eggshell paper business cards. Mr. Logan took one and put it in his shirt pocket.

"If everything checks out and Les wants to take part, he'll call you. You remember the directions?" Mr. Logan asked.

"Perfectly. Take care Larry and you too Les. Hope to hear from you soon. My word! The pollen count is high today," Professor Gluck said.

"That's what you get in Connecticut this time of year," Mr. Logan said and waved as Professor Gluck made it back to his car.

At the dinner table that night, Mr. Logan turned his attention to Les as he scooped potato salad onto his plate.

"He checks out. So you want to take him up on it?" Mr. Logan asked.

"That money would pay for your trip to the comic convention and maybe be enough to get you the new digital drawing tablet," Mrs. Logan said as she sat and then scooted her chair in close.

A yellow jacket outside the window kept bouncing off the glass and Les stared at the insect for a moment. He wiped his mouth with his napkin and looked at his plate.

"Not going to the con but the money would be nice. And, doesn't sound very hard," Les said.

"I say take it. And if it gets problematic, then quit," Mr. Logan said.

"All right," Les said.

Mr. Logan pulled out the business card and handed it to Les who crammed it in his pocket as he grabbed a piece of fried chicken and sunk his teeth through the crisp skin with a crunch. A nudge from Wooly Bully's cold nose left a wet spot on Les's leg under the table. Wooly Bully snorted to get his attention.

"No people food for you Wooly," Les said.

Dinner passed with smiles and conversations about the town installing windmills on the landfill. A work call then made Mr. Logan excuse himself. Les cleared the table and stacked the dishes in the sink as Wooly Bully sat on the cool tile floor.

"Mom, I'll put the dishes in the dishwasher later. I need to go check my messages," Les said.

"Just run it before bed. Electricity is cheaper late at night," Mrs. Logan said.

The click clack of Wooly Bully's footsteps carried up the stairs while he followed Les into his room. On the bed, Les's phone glowed.

"What the..? Crap phone on the fritz again. Definitely taking the job so I can get a Droid or an iPhone and toss that POS Wooly."

The phone then rang with a plain ring tone. Les thought he had it set to vibrate. The phone flipped open with a snap and he read the number of the dialer.

"Jerk wants to play, fine," he said.

Les's face became a snarl and he hit the answer button.

"Think you can harass me? I called the cops punk. Tracing this back as we speak," Les said.

He expected a laugh, a yell, a muffled sick reply but an odd static pulsed in his ear. Then, the static broke.

"No, you didn't. Listen L. I need help and don't have much time to explain. My minutes will be up soon. You need to help me," the voice from the phone said.

Les began scratching his knee, a tick he thought long gone, and he looked over to Wooly Bully who twisted his head to look back with sleep rich eyes. The voice was Aki's and Les knew it.

"Is that you?"

"Yes. It's me. Sorry I haven't been able to call before but figuring out this ghost thing is weird," Aki said.

Les's hair tingled and his eyes refused to blink.

"Okay, if it's you what's the hero's name?

"Janus."

"No way."

"Listen dip-shit, it's me. I've been trying to get your attention for days. And yes, there's life after death, but like the movies say if you got unfinished business you can't move on. Thing is you don't have unlimited time. I have like seven minutes of calls," Aki said.

"I can't believe it?"

"That is why you fail," Aki said.

"An Empire reference, it is you."

"First off, fix Bob. And second I need help," Aki said.

"What can I possibly do?" Les said.

"You need to find Rachel Higgs in Clover," Aki said.

"Clover, the town?"

"Yes, the town a few miles away. Focus dude, Rachel got my liver after the accident and won't get on with her life. She has a part of me and I have to make sure everything is okay before I become one with the force and move to the bright side. You must get a message to her," Aki said.

"Is it really like the force?"

"No, well sort of, listen L, I have only a few more seconds on this call. Find her and help her. You're my only hope," Aki said and the phone went silent. Les looked at the phone and the display was dark.

"So I'm off on some damn fool crusade. Why do I have to be Obi Wan? I'll probably have to pay Mr. Lucas just for saying that Wooly. Wait. This can't be real. I'm hallucinating. Going nuts."

The phone rang.

"Hello," Les said.

"No you're not crazy and Obi Wan is great. He's the only hero throughout the entire epic, well besides R2. Gotta go. I'll be watching," Aki said and the phone once more went silent. A tear ran over a smile.

"Worst best day ever Wooly but how am I going to find Rachel Higgs? And I need help. But who would believe me?"

Chapter 7: A babe in the woods.

In order to help Aki and get a new phone, Les needed money so he decided to take the job with the professor while he tracked down Rachel Higgs in Clover. First he would call the Professor and then Eddie to discuss what happened. She was the only person he knew who had any knowledge about psychics and spirits. Eddie fancied herself intuitive and was trying to develop ESP skills ever since her aunt took her to a psychic fair upstate at Cherry Park where she had a Kirlian photograph taken. The picture showed a colorful aura surrounding her and she was told that it was called Electrography.

Les gulped, took a deep breath, and picked up the phone in his father's den. The business card with Professor's Gluck's number rested next to the phone on the short Ikea table that nestled beside Mr. Logan's green lounge chair. A trembling finger dialed. One ring resounded in his ear like a siren and then the call was answered.

"Hello," the professor said.

"Hello, Dr. Gluck?"

"Yes."

"This is Les Logan, I was calling to see if you still wanted me for the work?"

"Glad you called. Yes, I would very much like for you to be in the study and also do the chores. Are the terms agreeable?"

"You mean you'll pay me what you said?"

"Yes. Same pay rate."

"All right. What do you want me to do?"

"The study for the older group starts on Wednesday, it's when the summer session begins but we can start whenever we like. After that I just need you to come by once a week to garden and complete miscellaneous chores. Please be at my house on Tuesday at ten. My morning class is over at nine."

"The study isn't at a lab at Upton?"

"No, I have a home office where I'll conduct this study. I need a neutral environment and the college has too much stimuli."

"Oh, all right. I'll be at your house then."

"The first part of the study should take about two hours. My address is 101 Brookside Lane."

"I know where that is. I'll see you then Doctor Gluck."

"Excellent. And please call me Professor Gluck. I find the doctor title just gets in the way."

"Okay Professor Gluck."

"Okay Les. See you then."

In his second story computer room, Professor Gluck hung up the phone and smiled.

Les hung up the phone and cracked his neck. Wooly Bully bound into the den, and bowed like dogs do, ready to play. A cool draft tinted with the scent of popcorn then pushed across Les's face. An intrigued eyebrow rose up and Les waved for Wooly Bully to follow him as he slipped down the hall to the kitchen. The microwave oven chimed three times and Les heard the plastic door being yanked open. His mother pulled out a bag of popcorn from the microwave, holding it by the corners, as he entered. Mr. Logan was in the breakfast nook on his laptop.

"Would you like some popcorn?" Mrs. Logan asked.

"No, it gets stuck between my teeth. Wanted to tell you guys that I took the job with that weird professor," Les said, leaned against the countertop and scratched his knee.

A chair was pushed against the wall in the nook and Mr. Logan came into the kitchen with a smile that seemed to extend around his eyes and attach to his wrinkled forehead. Wooly Bully trotted over to Mrs. Logan and sat.

"Good to hear Les. So, you want to drive the Fiat to work?" Mr. Logan asked as he pulled his jean shorts higher on his waist.

"No, you know I can't drive that," Les said and scratched his other knee.

"How are you going to get there?" Mrs. Logan asked and opened the bag of popcorn at the edges to vent the steam.

"Skate."

"Where?" Mr. Logan asked.

"Brookside."

"It will take you thirty minutes to get there," Mr. Logan said.

"No biggie."

"You'll have to drive sometime Lester," Mrs. Logan said and poured the popcorn into a ceramic bowl painted with daffodils and violets.

"Sometime yes. Just not now."

"Well, figuring out a commute will help you with your time management skills that you so desperately need to refine," Mr. Logan said.

"Why do you have to make everything sound like business dad? Geez," Les asked.

"Because son, you are seventeen and soon everything will be," Mr. Logan said.

"No, not everything is about business Dad," Les said.

"True, but you understand what I mean. Even with your art and comics, you have to make a living," Mr. Logan said.

"I know Dad. I'm not even in college yet. Just, never mind…" Les said and pushed off the countertop.

A quick hand waved for Wooly Bully to follow but the dog stayed right next to his mother and looked up with puppy eyes.

"Food always wins, doesn't it," Les said and went to his room.

On an unmade bed, Les sat, picked up his cell phone and stared. No call.

"All right Aki, I'll try to find this Rachel. Why don't you call and tell me how? I need more info," Les said.

No call came so he got up and placed the phone on the desk next to the keyboard.

"This is nuts, not even sure if it's real or if that pill messed me up forever. Look at me. I must be crazy talking to myself."

His chair wobbled as he sat. Through his window, Les saw the sun being covered by pewter clouds. The computer's fan began to hum and Les went on-line. The still potent scent of lemon Pledge floated off his dresser from when his mother insisted he clean it hours ago.

His homepage resolved and he plugged in Rachel Higgs, Clover, transplant, into the search engine. Thousands of matches came up but only one perfect match. The cursor clicked on the monitor and Rachel Higgs's Facebook profile flooded his LCD screen. Her photo hung in the left corner and thick dark curls spiraled down her heart shaped face. Everything else was locked out. No access.

"Pretty. Guess I have to try and friend her but let's see what else."

Les clicked out after sending a friend request. The search engine was pulled back up and he typed: liver transplant. Rachel Higgs. The first link was to an article in his local paper, The Hour. He clicked and read she was a senior at Burr High School, worked at Carvel ice cream, sang and played the guitar in a band. Then Les came upon the heart of the story. It said she had a disease called Biliary Atresia that blocked her bile ducts and had the first surgery on her liver when she was only five weeks old. One doctor quoted said he was surprised that her liver lasted as long as it did but a transplant was inevitable.

There was no contact information, no address, but the reporter had an email address. Les figured if she didn't friend him, he would contact the reporter with some story about how he wanted to learn about transplants, and he honestly did want to know about them since learning about organ donation before getting his driver's license. He read more stories and interviews he found posted by transplant patients.

A buzz permeated his room as the phone rattled on the desk. Panic drenched Les. It could be Aki. He answered without looking.

"Hello."

"Hi L. What's up?" Eddie asked.

"Eddie, oh it's you, not much."

"You sound surprised," she said.

"Oh. What's up?"

"Wanted to see if you wanted to come with me tonight to party at the Cascades?" Eddie asked.

"P.J. coming?"

"No, he's doing something with his parents in the morning so he can't come out. But I heard Arden was going to be there," Eddie said.

"You know I'm not feeling her right now," Les said.

"Oh you are. You just don't want to admit it," Eddie said.

"What ev. I'm down. So the Cascades huh? Haven't been to the lake since last summer. What time?"

"Seven thirtyish," Eddie said.

"Cool. Hey, you're aunt is like a psychic right?"

"Yeah but you know I'm touched too right?" she said.

"Sure, I know. You know what, I'll tell you later," Les said.

"Tell me what later," Eddie said.

"Later."

Seven thirty on the dot, Eddie pulled up in Biggie Blue. The engine idled with a deep churning tumble of noise that boiled through the street. Her hair tied up with a black and white polka dot ribbon stood strong against the growing breeze. The car horn blared with three short blasts. Les hauled out of the front door, oversized t-shirt falling off his bones, and Wooly Bully came tumbling out after. He turned to see the dog gain on him and he stopped. His hand went up.

"No Wooly. Inside," Les said.

Wooly Bully ran by and leapt into the air and landed with a thud in the back seat of Biggie Blue. The tongue came out and Eddie twisted to yell, but before she could get anything out, Wooly Bully had slobber all over her chin. She couldn't help but laugh as the dog's frenzied licking tickled her face. Les rushed over, yanked open the heavy door, and grabbed Wooly Bully by the collar.

"Come on buddy. Eddie gets mad if you mess with her makeup," Les said.

The dog got in one final lick and Les pushed the front seat forward so the dog had a path. Wooly Bully took the opening as Mrs. Logan came out through the front door, martini in hand, while the watery ink of night spread in thin stokes across the orange moon above. She whistled and then took a sip of her drink. The dog's ears perked up and Les rubbed the dog's back.

"Go."

The dog sprinted by Mrs. Logan and went straight inside. Through the front window, Les could see the dog jump up onto the couch in the living room and smile a mischievous crooked grin as he sat like a person on the cushion. It reminded Les of Wooly Bully's face when they found him at the animal shelter four months ago. He remembered the dog cramped in a wire cage quite well. He remembered too many things well.

"Come on L, before spaz dog comes out again and follows us five miles like when I picked you up for the Biggie Blue test drive," she said.

With a hop and a push of the pedal, they were off into the wilds of the teenage night where potential lies hidden in every shadow and every encounter. The traffic was light going through downtown. Hardly a pedestrian strolled on the sidewalks. The bistros and taverns along the streets, all lit well, clad in brick and glass, clung to their corners as the traffic lights swayed in the summer breeze. The street lamps bent over the curbs like black candy canes out of season and each went on one at a time as the day retreated. A few cars Les recognized drove by that were plugged with teenagers but Eddie didn't honk or try to get their attention. She just drove.

In the curvy back roads, Les and Eddie plowed through the darkness with only the headlights to show them the way. They were only a few miles away from the Cascades, a lake and river system surrounded by pristine woods owned by the local water utility company. She rolled her fingers along the steering wheel with hard taps and shot a quick glance at Les.

"Yo. L. What were you going to tell me?" Eddie asked.

"Oh that. You believe in spirits right?"

"Of course, I've seen them. You know that."

"But you can't talk to them can you?"

"No, I haven't developed my gift to that point but my aunt can," Eddie said.

"Thought so. I think I believe now too," Les said and looked at the dash board.

"You? Really?"

"Yup and I think Aki contacted me."

She slammed on the breaks, the headlights panned across the rural road, and the blue car skid to a halt.

"What? What did you say?" Eddie asked.

"He called me. He called me on my cell phone."

"When? Why didn't you tell me earlier?"

"Thought I was going crazy," Les said and looked to the moon overhead.

"Some people will tell you that but you're not. What'd he say?" she asked.

"I have to help someone so he can go to the next level I guess," Les said.

"Who?"

"The girl who got his liver," Les said and he then looked down to Eddie.

"No way. I had a dream about that like two weeks ago," Eddie said.

"You said your aunt was full on psychic, can we go talk with her? I want to see if I can contact him without him calling me. Get more info," Les said.

"I'll call her when we get to the Cascades," Eddie said.

"Cool."

In a few moments, they pulled into a small gravel lot by an entrance to a hiking trail the cops never checked. From the rise, they could see across the lake that was spotted with white ripples in the growing breeze. At the other end of the lake, the main parking lot to the beach was filled with cars. They looked at each other and Les shook his head.

"Rookies. They're going to get pinched by the Po Pos over there," Les said.

"No doubt," Eddie said.

"So you don't think I'm crazy?" Les asked.

"No. You two were buds, connected, and if Aki needed help he'd come to you. Go on to the Slab, I'll catch up. Going to call my aunt," Eddie said.

"Sure? It's getting dark," Les said.

Eddie lifted her phone up and touched the screen. It flowed with light and illuminated her bare forearms. A mosquito struck into the column of blue light.

"Lamp," Eddie said.

"Cool, see you up there," Les said.

With quick steps, Les made his way through the shadows and onto to the thin trail. Over the ridge, a camp fire beckoned Les and spread its soft light through the deepening night that cut through the trees. He checked his pocket. The phone was there. An itch rose up on his kneecap but he refused to scratch and leaves scuffs of white patchy skin on his knees. Even if it was dark, he didn't want people to see evidence of his nervous tick.

The main river that fed Lake Pequot in the Cascade Park system hissed and churned down below the edge of the trail. Les was reminded of how Aki and he would take boogie boards and raft downstream into the lake from the Crapper, a section of eroded bedrock where the current cut a smooth hole in the shape of the toilet bowel into the exposed stone. Les stuffed his hands in his pockets and waddled down the trail to a narrow foot path that led over to the Slab, a natural stone platform lined with a tight pebble beach. Across the Slab by the river, Luna and Arden stood in the flicker of campfire light and sipped from plastic cups.

The rush of the river created a white noise that masked the sound of the scenic highway a few miles away but not the chatter of teenagers, a few nearby frogs, and the buzz of mosquitoes that flew by unsuspecting ears. Les tilted his chin down and shuffled over towards Luna and Arden. Chuck, a guy Les played hockey with, extended his hand as Les walked by the fire. Les stopped and shook his hand.

"Hey bro, haven't seen you much," Chuck said.

"Yeah, I'm tapped for cash so I'm not out much," Les said.

"I know that. There's a keg over by the bend if you want," Chuck said.

"Thanks bro," Les said and they shook again.

"You ever lace up and get on the ice? You were good. Should try out again," Chuck said.

"No, probably won't. You guys had two years to get stronger. Couldn't keep up now," Les said.

"You're fine. Just hit the weights," Chuck said.

"Maybe. Got to go. Nice seeing you bro," Les said.

Chuck nodded with a wide grin as he raised his plastic cup to his lips.

Warm beer wasn't inviting to Les and he didn't want to risk being caught drinking. The last time he drank was after Aki's funeral and it ended with him hugging a real toilet bowl and not the Crapper. As Les ventured closer to Luna and Arden, he accidentally kicked a rock. It launched through the air and cracked Luna right in the shin.

Chapter 8: A flash of lights.

"I'm so sorry. Didn't mean to do that. Sorry," Les said as Luna was bent over rubbing her shin. She looked up at him like he was diseased.

"Watch it. You're like cursed or something," Luna said.

Les's face dropped.

"But, I'm…" Les said and Luna walked away with an exaggerated limp.

Chuck saw her hobbling and rushed to Luna's side. Arden laughed and shook her head. Her hands went over her mouth as she tried to muffle the sound but her laugh got louder and seeped through her fingers. The world seemed heavier to Les. It pushed him down but he managed to look over at Arden. She lowered her hands and stopped shaking her head.

"You always find a way to injure her. I remember when you pushed her on the swing in elementary school and she slipped off and fell onto the pavement," Arden said.

"I don't remember that," Les said.

"She does. Do you remember at your hockey game when you hit her in the bleachers with a puck?" Arden asked.

"No one told me about that," Les said.

"That's delish," Arden said and twirled her hair.

A smile crouched around Les's face for a second but then sat when he remembered something. He remembered that Arden had been saying delish and twirling her hair since the fifth grade in Mr. Ostrander's class.

"Think she'll be okay?" Les asked.

"She's fine. Let her play poor me for a bit," Arden said.

She looked at Les with blushed cheeks that were visible even in the weak camp fire light.

"She sure has changed since we were friends," Les said.

"And like you haven't? You went from hockey jock to moody artist in like a year," Arden said.

"I broke my leg," Les said.

"I know. I signed the cast. So are you going to try to hook up with Luna?" Arden asked.

"Uh, I uh…" Les said.

"Never mind, that tells me everything. Did you know that in middle school she wrote LL plus LL in her notebook for like a year?" Arden asked.

"Our initials?"

"Duh," Arden said.

"Had no idea, but she's likes jocks and older dudes now," Les said.

"Yeah she does. Well, you had your chance," Arden said.

"With what?" Les asked.

Arden shrugged and walked away. She looked back over her shoulder at Les as she slipped away into the darkness. He then understood what she meant. When he was about to go after Arden, Eddie grabbed his shoulder from behind. He swung around.

"Tomorrow, we're going to my aunt's. I told her all about it and she wants to help," Eddie said.

"Cool. Thanks. Thanks for everything, especially believing me," Les said.

"Dude, what's up with you? You're being all squishy nice," Eddie asked.

"Uh nothing, think I blew my chances with two girls tonight," Les said.

"Wow, it's been like ten minutes," Eddie said.

"I'm good like that," Les said.

The mosquitoes bit and some people came and some people left. The party went on for an hour under the canopy of trees and night; the noise was hidden by the fast flowing waters and then flashlights came. Beams tracked across the trails and scanned the river. They got close. The flashlights bounced up and down through the thick underbrush and thick humid air.

"Cops!"

Everyone dropped their cups and scattered. Most went up the trail to reach the bridge so they could cross over to the other side of the lake and take the back trails to the main parking lot. Les ran back down the trail and when he took a corner his feet got snagged on a root. His hand braced him from the fall. A beam of light crossed above his head as he stayed flat on the dirt. He took a slow breath and held it.

Coming up around the curve in the path, the flashlight beam jumped from side to side and stopped on a boulder between gnarled tree stumps. Les exhaled as he saw the glimmer of a badge and crawled his way through a bush. Leaves crunched under his hands and Les froze. The flashlight swung at him. There was no escape.

"Freeze! Police."

The cop focused the light on Les's face and bore down on him.

"Get up," the cop said.

"Okay," Les said and pushed up to his feet and smacked his hands free of dirt.

"What are you doing? Where's the party?" the cop asked.

"What party I was just kicking around," Les said.

"On the ground? Who are you?" the cop asked.

"Les Logan, Lester Logan."

"You were the kid in the accident," the cop asked.

"Yeah."

"You been drinking?" the cop asked.

"No."

The cop stepped closer to Les and held his flashlight high as he sniffed the air.

"You don't smell like booze. So why are you here?" he asked.

"Like I said, kicking around. Sometimes I just go for walks to clear my head."

"Why were you on the ground?" the cop asked and stepped back.

"Didn't know who was chasing me so I ran and tripped on a root."

"The park closes at sundown. Get out of here," the cop said.

"Okay," Les said.

The cop walked up the trail towards the Slab so Les decided to get back to Biggie Blue as fast as he could. Through the side trail and around the bend, he made it back but Biggie Blue wasn't there. He pulled out his old phone and looked at the time.

"Well, I have two hours to walk home before curfew. Beat," Les said.

Down the stretch of rural road, Les walked with his hands in his pockets kicking loose chunks of asphalt as he pushed on through the slips of night. The gurgle and growl of a car engine chugged across the back of his neck from around the curve and headlights followed. Tires screeched.

"L, get in," Eddie said.

The next morning came with the sizzle of bacon perfuming the air and the chopping of a blade through melon on a cutting board echoed up to his room. He rolled to his nightstand and picked up his phone. He had twenty minutes until Eddie arrived at his house and two voice mails. One is from Aki's number.

"No way," Les said.

He looked down to the laundry covered floor where Wooly Bully was asleep on his back. Doggie dreams filled his head as his paws twitched and his lips quivered. The first message was answered.

"Hi L, she won't friend you. You have to go to Clover. I'll be in touch soon and Eddie is on the way," said Aki's voice.

"Crazy."

Les took a deep breath, slowly exhaled, and played the second message from Eddie.

"Be ready. And don't wear anything leather, my aunt's vegan. Says it messes up her gift. See ya."

Blurry eyes commanded Les to rub them so he did in soft circles. At his computer he went online and found Aki was right. She didn't friend him.

"Damn," Les said and a knock came from the door.

"Get some bacon before it gets cold," Mrs. Logan said through the door.

"All right Mom," Les said.

He sniffed the pile of clothes at the foot of his bed and found what he was looking for; his blue madras shorts and the Punisher t-shirt he ordered online that didn't smell. Wooly Bully woke up and perked up. An eager tail wagged and Les pet his head and went down stairs with Wooly Bully just inches behind. The dog gobbled up the kibble as Les poured it into his bowl.

Only two pieces of honeydew melon went down before Les heard the cry of Biggie Blue outside. He wiped his hands on a dish towel to his mother's dismay and rushed to the upstairs bathroom to gargle mouth wash. He heard his mother let Eddie in.

Leaning against the banister at the bottom of the stairs, Les saw Eddie with her arms crossed over her white blouse with a lace collar.

"Dude, I told you to be ready," Eddie said.

"Over slept and had to deal with my messages," Les said.

"Messages, really?" Eddie said.

"Tell you later."

Mrs. Logan stepped out from around the corner with a clean dish towel and a cutting board in hand. She dried the cutting board as she coughed, not a sick cough, a let me know cough.

"Shouldn't you be going to work by now?" Les asked.

"Flex hours, I'm going in at one. That means you and your father will be ordering pizza tonight. So where to?" Mrs. Logan asked.

"We're going to my aunt's house in New Lisbon. I want Les to meet her boyfriend. He's an artist," Eddie said.

"It's a little far, but have fun, and be careful. Call me if you need anything Hamster," Mrs. Logan said.

"Sure Mom. Sorry about that," Les said and Wooly Bully nudged him with his wet nose.

"Sorry Wooly Bully, but you can't come," Eddie said.

"I have to get ready," Mrs. Logan said and went back to the kitchen.

The rural four lane highway rumbled under Biggie Blue as Eddie and Les left the borders of New Hebron. The summer air was dense with the scent of honeysuckle and slants of sunlight angled through the trees bordering the open road. Les turned to Eddie and cleared his throat so he could talk over the road noise.

"Is your aunt's boyfriend really an artist?" Les asked.

"Yeah, but not like you. He's what I call and interactive performance artist but he does paint, sort of," Eddie said.

A pickup truck with a panel advertising Black Mountain Construction on the door rolled parallel with Biggie Blue. A sunburned man with a John Deere cap on his head winked at Eddie from the passenger window. She chuckled and shook her head. Les snickered and rolled his eyes. The man in the John Deere cap flicked his tongue. Eddie grabbed her phone from the drink holder and snapped a picture. The man's sunburned face went white.

"Got your bosses number jerk," Eddie yelled.

A flurry of slaps came from the drivers' side of the pickup truck and smacked the John Deere cap out the window. Biggie Blue pulled away as Les relaxed in the seat and chewed on his lower lip. He looked at Eddie.

"That was reckless funny. You get it a lot now that…?"

"Now that what?" Eddie asked and sneered.

"Not that… Now that you wear makeup and crap. The whole fifties look. You know?" Les said.

"Joking L. But yes, I get that a lot but probably because of my boobs," Eddie said.

"Sucks."

The wind whipped and tossed their hair as Biggie Blue came upon a flat stretch of highway basking under full sun. The traffic was thin and the exits got farther and farther away from each other as they headed north.

"L, you ever get advice from that editor on Twitter?" Eddie asked.

"Yeah, BlowpopPower is cool. She told me to network, go to cons and when I was done with Janus, one of the comics Aki and I were working on, to contact literary agents," Les said.

"When do you think you'll be done with Janus?"

"I'm not working on it anymore."

A tractor trailer blew its air horn as it passed by Biggie Blue and blocked the sun.

Up over the northern hills they drove and in an hour they pulled off the main road and entered the proper hamlet of New Lisbon. Three churches, two gas stations and one main street with cobblestones and brick clad shops pass them by. They turned down a private marl road lined with old growth hemlock. Gravel spat out from under Biggie Blue's tires as they pulled up in front of an expansive log cabin with a weathered deck that seemed to be attached to the hill the house sat on. The slope above and below the cabin was dense with majestic oaks and slippery elms. Three blasts from behind the house startled Les into the back of his seat.

"Don't worry Hamster, it's just a shotgun," Eddie said.

"Shotgun? Hamster?"

Chapter 9: Some things are strange and others, bizarre.

Les unbuckled his seatbelt and looked at Eddie with wide unblinking eyes.

"I knew we were in the boonies but shooting off shotguns in your yard is pretty messed up," Les said.

"It's how Balthazar paints. You'll see," Eddie said.

"What's a Balthazar?"

"My aunt's boyfriend. He's harmless. Weird but harmless," Eddie said and turned off the engine.

"That his real name?"

"No idea," Eddie said.

Her aunt Daisy sprung forth from the front door with arms spread wide to greet them. A purple ankle length dress clung to Daisy's legs as she descended the short set of stairs. A violet stuffed behind her ear, entangled in thick cords of auburn hair, was a contrast in light to her pallid complexion. Les thought she must be a hippie. He didn't trust hippies.

"My beautiful Edwina," Daisy said as she clapped her hands together and then lifted her fingertips to her lips.

"Hi, this is L. L this is my aunt Daisy," Eddie said.

"Hi," Les said.

As he got out of the car, Les was surprised that Daisy came over and hugged him. His face cringed for a second as he held his arms out and just took the hug.

"So you are the blessed one. Wonderful. I do hope we can reach your friend. Come inside to the parlor," Daisy said.

Two shotgun blasts echoed around the house. Les shook the impact off.

"Is that legal," Les asked.

"Oh yes. We have permits and our nearest neighbor is a mile away," Daisy said.

They headed for the porch and Les cupped his ears just in case. The warped steps creaked and bent under Les' weight as he climbed up to the front door.

Daisy held the door open.

"He's painting again?" Eddie asked.

"He's creating dear," Daisy said.

Inside, they passed by an empty room with a cement floor on their way to a spiral staircase. Les followed Eddie up the helix.

They walked through a narrow hall with exposed log walls and by a finished yoga studio to a parlor. Wow it really was a parlor, Les thought.

In the unfinished room of wood beams, couches sat at right angles to each other on a rough cut floor. A paisley chaise lounge sprawled in the center of the room where wooden stools dotted the foot and plump red bean-bag chairs were scattered about. A bay window like a massive lens allowed the forest canopy to creep into view, green and bright. Daisy closed the door behind them.

Les sniffed the air. The room smelled of pine, burnt leaves and wet charcoal. He was reminded of when he, P.J and Aki went camping and their camp fire got drench from an unexpected storm. Les found the culprit as he scanned the room. A small fireplace was wedged in the far side of the parlor that sat between two bookshelves that had no books.

Daisy bowed. Les looked to Eddie and she gave him a jerky nod to sit. They sat on a checkered couch and Daisy sat cross legged on a Navajo blanket covering the rough wood floor. She spun a turquoise ring on her left index finger.

"Les, tell me what you wish?" Daisy asked.

"I want to talk to my friend Aki and know specifically what he needs me to do," Les said.

"Edwina told me. It is a wonderful thing and I think I can help. But, you must trust me," Daisy said.

"Okay," Les said but thought weird.

"Do you have the portal?" Daisy asked.

"The phone?" Les asked.

"Yes, it is the portal or medium that allows communication," Daisy said.

"Right here," Les said.

He pulled the phone out of his shorts pocket and handed it to her. With diligent eyes, Daisy examined the phone back to front and opened it.

"May I?" she asked while holding her finger on the recent calls menus.

"Go ahead," Les said.

Daisy hit the button and scrolled through the calls.

"Edwina said his name is Aki, yet I don't see any numbers with that name," Daisy said.

"What? Can't be. I didn't delete them. Please," Les said and stretched out his hand.

He went through the list and Aki's number didn't come up. He checked his voice mails and the messages were gone. A confused expression scoured across Les's face.

"I don't understand," he said.

"Don't worry. Spirits are great at not being seen when they don't want to be, but it doesn't mean they aren't there. Do you feel anything Edwina? You knew the departed," Daisy asked and spun the ring.

"It's thin but there. No contact though," Eddie said.

"Ah, let's join hands and see if I can summon him," Daisy said.

They joined hands. A thick cloud covered the sun leaving darkness behind in the parlor.

"Close your eyes," Daisy said.

They closed their eyes in unison. The cloud moved on returning the light to the room that smelled even more strongly of charcoal to Les than before.

"Dear Aki, come forth and let your presence be known. Your friends wish to speak with you and discover what you need," Daisy said.

A shotgun blast echoed outside rattling the bay window. Daisy opened her eyes.

"Hold on," Daisy said and got up.

She went to a small casement window, cranked it open and put her head out.

"B-zar, I'm trying to help my niece's friend. It's the séance I told you about. Could you please refrain for a few moments?" Daisy asked.

A smile grew on her face.

"Thank you," she said and sat back down on the blanket.

"I thought his name was Balthazar?" Eddie asked.

"B-zar is a nickname his mother gave him when he got lost in a Moroccan Bizarre. Now let's try again. Hold hands and close your eyes," Daisy said.

Les doubted that was why he had such a nickname. They held hands and closed their eyes.

"Dear Aki please come through. Make your presence known. Move an object, use the phone, please come to us," Daisy said.

Nothing happened.

"Dear Aki, your friends want to help you. Please make your presence known," Daisy said.

The door flew open and gust of air flowed over them. They opened their eyes and standing at the door was a dark presence. It stepped into the light. There, Balthazar stood with his head bowed and he was dressed in green army fatigues splattered with paint. He lurched forward and stared at Les. With a quick glance, Les looked up at him and saw a man with four eyes. Real eyes sat atop a pair of eyes tattooed in black and blue ink on his cheekbones.

"Greeting, can I help with the séance?" Balthazar asked.

"Certainly, but you know your training isn't complete so don't try to summon," Daisy said.

Balthazar walked over to the couch with his toes facing out like a duck. He bent down beside Eddie.

"Hello Edwina," he said and kissed her on the cheek.

She turned away with annoyed, narrow eyes. Balthazar shot his hand out. Les grabbed it and squeezed tight as they shook. He was told by his father to always have a firm handshake. Balthazar's hand was weak in Les's grasp.

"You must be L. Great to meet a fellow artist," He said.

"Sure man," Les said.

Daisy cleared her throat. Balthazar put his hands up in a defensive posture and snuck behind Daisy and sat on the exposed wood floor.

"Let us try again. Everyone close your eyes. This time we will not bind ourselves and each of us will draw in Aki's spirit with happy memories of him. Think of those memories now," Daisy said.

Les didn't know if he could recall a happy memory because every time he thought of Aki, he saw the crash, but he would try.

"Aki please let your presence be known," Daisy said.

The wind picked up outside and sent a downdraft through the chimney sending a whistle across the room. The scent of soggy charcoal became stronger and irritated Eddie's nose until she sneezed.

"Bless you," Les said eyes still closed.

"Sorry," Eddie said eyes still closed.

"Could be a sign," Balthazar said.

Les's phone rang.

All eyes opened and Les looked at the number.

"Sorry, it's my mother," Les said.

After Les talked to his mother, a reminder call about feeding Wooly Bully dinner when he got home, the séance continued uninterrupted and uneventful for the next hour through a series of Sanskrit chants and Native American invocations. Unsuccessful, they resigned to the porch to recline on black wrought iron patio furniture covered in speckles of white paint.

"Please don't be discouraged Les. The spirits have their own will and when they want to speak they shall," Daisy said.

Eddie checked her phone for messages.

"I really am stuck," Les said, swatted a fly away and continued, "my proof is gone. And I came thinking it would be easy to contact Aki but no," Les said.

"Easy, L? Nothing that is great is easy. And something great already happened. Why do you need any more proof?" Eddie said.

"I could be nuts," Les said.

"Do you believe you talked to your friend?" Daisy asked.

"Yes, I think so. Sounded real," Les said.

"Did he ask you to hurt anyone or do anything that could hurt you?" Daisy asked.

"No, he wanted me to help someone," Les said.

"Then help someone. Honor his wishes and even if he didn't contact you, you honor his memory," Daisy said.

Les thought she was right.

"I'm going to help. I already started but I guess I was just looking for more answers," Les said.

"Good," Daisy said.

"Looking for answers means you have questions. That's good. Very adult. When you give of yourself, that's when you are most human," Balthazar said.

"Thanks for trying," Les said to Daisy.

"Glad to be of service. Edwina, how are your remote viewing exercises coming along?" Daisy asked.

"Okay. I was able to see the train station where you left the target box. Mom said it took her a month before she could," Eddie said.

"Excellent, your gift is stronger than mine at your age," Daisy said.

"Listen, I hate to ask Balthazar, but…" Les tried to finish but Balthazar stood up and pointed to his eye tattoos.

"I got the Eyes of Isis ink to remind me that I must always keep my eyes open to new experiences. Even when we sleep, we must be searching. Would you like to go around back and do some dynamic painting?" he asked.

"What's that?" Les asked but knew what the answer was.

"Painting with shotguns. I hang zip-lock bags of paint from a tree limb and put a canvas behind. Then I let gravity, gunpowder and lead do the rest," Balthazar said.

Eddie shot Les a glance. He also knew what that meant.

"No, but thanks. Thank you both. I actually have to get going. Starting a job tomorrow and I have chores," Les said and stood.

Eddie stood and went over to Daisy.

"Thanks. By the way, Mom's birthday is Wednesday and I'm cooking. Will you'll be there?" Eddie asked her aunt.

"Of course we'll be there," Daisy said and embraced her niece with a tight hug. They rocked in the sunlight until Daisy let go and then turned to Les.

"Your friend is listening. And I'm sorry I couldn't be of any more help," Daisy said.

"I found what I needed. Thanks. Nice meeting you B-zar," Les said.

"Likewise, keep creating," Balthazar said.

"Thanks. Bye."

Down the rolling four-lane highway, separated by ditches and guardrails, Biggie Blue rumbled with Eddie and Les back towards the coast, back towards New Hebron. Les was happy to just listen to the wind huff in his ear. The silence between them didn't bother Les but Eddie smacked a glancing blow across Les's shoulder.

"What'd I do?" Les asked and rubbed his shoulder even though it didn't hurt.

"Nothing. I'm proud of you. You opened your mind to new experiences and didn't stare at Balthazar," she said.

"That took all of my strength. All of it," Les said.

"He's kind of weird isn't he?" Eddie asked.

"Unique. He's unique. Nah, he puts Mariah Carey and Britney Spears to shame," Les said and laughed.

Eddie's smile practically wrapped around her head and before they knew it they pulled up in front of the Logan household. Wooly Bully was having a barking fit in the window.

"Got to go, but thanks Eddie, I mean it," Les said

"I know. Hey, I just had a crazy idea. Why don't you call Aki's number?" Eddie asked.

Chapter 10: Questions and questionnaires.

The coils of Les's bed creaked as he flipped on his back and stared through the thin beams of darkness that were topped with triangles of dirty light coming through his window from the street. The crickets had begun their serenade and the frogs from the nearby pond croaked a counter melody but these weren't the only things keeping Les up. He had to work in the morning but he had to know.

The edge of a headlight from a passing car tracked through his room as it took the far corner down the street. Les puffed his cheeks as he blew out a slow exhale. The phone was on the nightstand. The number dialed. One ring fell across his ear.

"L, you shouldn't waste your minutes," Aki said.

"I can call you?"

"Yeah, duh. Dude, listen we can't waste minutes but here's the four-one-one. Can't get to the bright side until Rachel gets out of her shell and on with her life. She can't waste the cells I gave her," Aki said.

"I will find her. Help her."

"I knew you would bro, but you need to know we don't have much time," Aki said.

"Why?"

"Two reasons. One is she needs to make a choice before it can't be made anymore and second that's my deadline, no pun intended. I'll disintegrate when the last of my minutes are used up. If she doesn't get on with her life, poof, I'm done. Or at least that's what I could find out from a whole bunch of weird crap that's happened," Aki said.

"Why did you delete the messages?"

"I didn't want to talk to them, Eddie yes, but not her aunt. She would have done what you did. Call and that would waste our minutes. Speaking of, they are running out and when they're done, they're done," Aki said.

"I'll get help and I'll find her. By the way dude, she's hot," Les said.

"So death was the only way I was going to be with a hot chick huh?" Aki asked.

"Funny dude. Question. Did it hurt? Are you in pain?" Les asked.

"Dying hurt a little to be honest but when you're dead you don't feel pain. There are other things but not pain. It's like being one step out of phase with reality in a Star Trek episode. Now get some sleep so you can make some easy cheddar. I have limited amount of time to talk so don't call me. I'll call you," Aki said.

"I'm sorry bro."

"I know."

. . .

The bow of the night broke and the cradle of morning fell. Wooly Bully sat by his food dish as Mrs. Logan stirred her coffee.

"Go get Les, Wooly. He'll feed you," she said.

Ears perked up, feet lifted, dog claws clacked on the hardwood floors up the stairs and down to Les's door that was ajar. A black nose wedged in the space and Wooly Bully pushed the door open. With a strong jump, he cleared Les and hopped up to his face where a doggie tongue smacked Les's ear.

"I'm up pup. Down, down," Les said and looked at his clock.

He had two hours and needed to skate over. Wooly Bully plopped his forelegs across Les's chest waited to be petted. Wooly Bully got his wish, both of them.

The dog bowl was cleaned by a fast chomping Wooly Bully as Mr. and Mrs. Logan sat in the breakfast nook. Les wondered why his father was still there as he grabbed an apple and went in with Wooly Bully right behind.

"Why you home?"

"Flex time. Have some stuff I can do from here," Mr. Logan said.

"Cool. Maybe you can give me a ride to the Professor's?" Les asked.

"Ah yes, I was wondering why you were up. No, I can't give you a ride, but you can take my car and I'll take the Fiat to work," Mr. Logan said.

Mr. Logan expected a yes.

"No I'll skate," Les said.

"That's an awfully long distance," Mrs. Logan said.

"Not really. I'm out," Les said and took a bite of the apple.

"Fine. One step at a time then. Have a good day Les. Remember, we love you," Mr. Logan said.

"Yeah I know. Mom could you distract Wooly when I leave? I don't want him getting loose and following me," Les said.

"Okay Hamster," Mrs. Logan said.

"Mom, please don't call me Hamster."

"Lester, you will always be my little hamster. You're lucky I don't say it in front of your friends all the time," Mrs. Logan said.

"And she wants to, oh she wants to Les, so let your mother call you Hamster or… It's your choice," Mr. Logan said and bit his lip to contain his laughter.

"Bye," Les said, bit his apple and prepared for the day.

The wheels of Les's skateboard rattled on the old asphalt of the side street as they attacked the groves and pits in the road until he reached slick new blacktop. The wheels met the smooth surface and silenced. He pumped his legs and rolled down the even street. A fast moving gallop of what Les could only think was from a neighbor's dog called him to look over his shoulder. A dog barreled down the road at him and a spike of adrenaline pricked his skin. He looked closer. Wooly Bully was loose.

The skateboard ground to a stop and Les puts his hands out.

"Heel Wooly," Les said and saw a car barreling at them.

He hopped off the board and ran to the dog who dodged him with play in his eyes. The collar slipped from Les's grasp as the car got closer. The bass beats coming from the car's overpowered stereo thudded against the suburban landscape. Wooly Bully jumped to the side and Les just grabbed him with both arms. He dragged Wooly Bully to the curb as he squirmed and almost slipped away. The car went by and struck his skateboard sending it spinning into a tree. The driver didn't look. The driver did not stop.

The collar firm in hand, Les walked Wooly Bully over to his splintered deck. He inspected the wreckage.

"Damn it. That's going to cost. At least the trucks are fine."

Back the way he came, Les and Wooly Bully went home. His parents didn't know Wooly Bully was even loose and Les had no time to argue so he grabbed a pair of shoes and his old roller blades that haven't been used for months. They still fit so off he went, shoes in hand, back down the even streets under the unwavering sunny day. To his surprise, the blades felt good on his feet and he made better time to the professor's house on Brookside Lane than he thought.

On the cement curb outside Professor Gluck's house, Les sat and took off the roller blades. He glanced over his shoulder for a moment and looked up to the shiny copper roof.

"Nice. Must be new."

He slipped on the pair of Adidas Sambas he carried from home and watched as a group college girls in tight shorts stroll by. He thought that college couldn't come fast enough and walked up the slate walkway to the door. Les knocked three times. Lazlo yanked back the door and stared at Les with almond shaped eyes.

"Les right?" Lazlo asked.

"Yup."

"I'm Lazlo. Follow me and don't touch anything," he said.

"Cool," Les said, lifted up his roller blades, and asked, "where do I put these?"

"Just carrying them with you. You have a space downstairs," Lazlo said.

"Okay."

The house was museum clean and quiet but the smell reminded Les of his grandmother's room at the convalescence home, stale with ammonia. Through the dark house they walked. Les held his roller blades high so not to bump into anything as they passed by a white tiled kitchen. It was the emptiest kitchen he had ever seen. There was nothing but space. The white tile amplified the hum of the old refrigerator. They came to a yellow door in a cramped hall marked "Subjects Only" on a makeshift sign held up by black tape.

They descended down sharp angled stairs to a basement finished with wood paneling and Lazlo waved Les on until they reached a door marked "Cell-17". Inside the closet sized room was a fold out table where a pencil and a stack of papers lined up with the corners. A single light burned overhead. A single chair sat below.

"Sit, fill out the questionnaire and the professor will be down to see you in a few. Don't lie on the questions, even the weird ones. It's confidential so nobody will ever know and we need you to be truthful. Plus, you're going to be asked the questions again at the end of the study. Oh yeah, turn off your cell phone," Lazlo said and shut Les in.

As Les sat, he felt a rush of cold air come over him and he thought he heard a voice, but when he listened there was nothing. The questionnaire was filled with odd questions, but Les filled it out as truthfully as he could and came upon a series of five questions under the heading Temporal Lobe activation study section. Supernatural: 1) Have you ever seen a UFO? Les checked the No box. 2) Do you believe Bigfoot exists? Les checked the No box. 3) Do you believe in an afterlife? Les hesitated, chewed on the eraser of the pencil, and check the Yes box. He figured lots of people do. 4) Have you ever seen a ghost? Les was torn. But he technically never saw Aki so he checked the No box. But then he read question five. He read it over and over. Les didn't want to tell anyone but Lazlo said he would be asked again so he decided to tell the truth. 5) Have you ever tried to talk to the dead? Les checked the Yes box since a lot of people talk to dead loved ones at grave sites.

What Les didn't know was that a tiny camera in the light above was watching him all along. At the viewing monitor in the second story computer room Professor Gluck clapped his hands together.

"I knew it Lazlo. He even hesitated on question four as well. I knew it. He's the one," Professor Gluck said.

"I hope so because you know what the dean said about publishing soon," Lazlo said.

"I am all too aware of 'Publish or Perish' Lazlo. It's him though. I feel it. Get the God helmet ready for a few tests and check the magnetic coils. If we can get him to summon his ghost friend, we can trap it in the cell phone matrix with the electro-magnetic bubble and then we will be the most famous men in science. Never will we have to worry about grants again," Professor Gluck said and touched the corners of his huge smile.

"I hope so. I'll be fast tracked on the PhD program and then all the cute lab assistants will want me," Lazlo said.

"We're about to make the greatest scientific discovery ever and you're thinking about sex. How driven by biology you are? Enough of this, I have to go talk to him," Professor Gluck said and stomped out the door.

Three knocks made Les look up. He put down his pencil. "Come on in," Les said.

The door swung open to allow the hall light to enter and there was a beaming Professor Gluck. Les thought it odd that he should be smiling like that.

"Hello Les," Professor Gluck said.

"Hi Professor Gluck," Les said and picked up the pencil.

"Done yet?" Professor Gluck asked.

"Almost. A few more," Les said.

"Good, good, take your time this is just a preliminary event. No rush. When you are done just leave the papers there and meet me outside at the garage will you?" Professor Gluck asked.

"Be there in a sec," Les said.

The door closed and Les finished.

Without Lazlo to guide him, and he was thankful for that, Les wandered up stairs and looked around to see what made this Professor tick. In a room that looked like a den, a TV sat on the floor unconnected to any cable box or satellite receiver and there was a single spindle back chair. The next room over had nothing but electronic equipment, spools of cable, and a few metal detectors. Les thought this all seemed very strange, especially the stale smell that lingered everywhere he stood.

Figuring the professor was just some absent minded scientist, Les made it out a side door and down the driveway to the open garage where the professor was inspecting a weed whacker like it was made of alien technology. Les placed his roller blades on the pavement.

"Oh, there you are. This here will be your assistant," Professor Gluck said and handed him the weed whacker.

"My dad makes me do that every week," Les said.

"Brilliant, then no instruction is needed. As you can see the lawn was mowed so just line the driveway and the backyard," Professor Gluck said, turned, pointed across the shady backyard and continued, "over there is a patch of strawberries that the birds seem to be getting at. If you could weed that area and put the plastic netting over the plants that should be it for this weeks gardening. The netting is in the back of the garage by the shovels and such."

"Cool, uh I hate to ask this. I busted my deck, uh sorry, my skateboard and need to get a new one. If you wouldn't mind paying me for the yard work this week and for the study that would be really cool. I promise I won't skip out," Les said.

"I will pay you for the weeding but I can't pay you for the entire study right now," Professor Gluck said.

"Damn, that's going to screw up my schedule cause I'll have to look for another job too," Les said.

He saw the professor's cheek quiver.

"How about half now and half when you're done?"

"That'd be cool," Les said.

"I'll need you to come back tomorrow after I process your information. I'll have the money then. Sorry I don't have it on me now but we in academia don't get paid as much as people think," Professor Gluck said.

"Awesome. I'll get to work," Les said and he yanked the starter cord to the weed whacker. The professor nodded and went inside. It didn't take long for Les to finish the driveway and move onto the backyard.

Up on the second floor, Lalzo put his earphones on as he tried to sift through data on other potential targets just in case Les didn't work out. The professor appeared in the door. The earphones came off and fell limp around his neck. The sound of an idle two stroke weed whacker engine bounced through the room. Lazlo spun in his office chair and shut the window. He sniffed the air in disgust.

"Ugh, smells awful. Couldn't you've have waited for him to do that later Gluck?" Lazlo asked.

"Don't get so familiar with me. I do what I do and you do what I tell you. Did you get any reading while he was in the room?" Professor Gluck asked.

"Not really any clear indications of defined or manifested EM fields but there was some activity when he was answering the questions about the supernatural," Lazlo said.

"Interesting. Anything on the audio recorders?"

"I'll pull it up now. Might be hard to hear with the racket outside," Lazlo said.

"That is why you have those things on your head."

"Oh."

Lazlo played through the recording and heard something. He took off the earphone with wide eyes and a wrinkled brow that told the professor all he needed to know.

"Give them here," Professor Gluck said and untangled them from Lazlo.

All went silent for the professor. The noise of the day slipped way. Then he heard it through a muffle of static hissing.

"L turn on your phone. L, turn on your phone."

The professor did not blink. He stepped back to the wall and the chord ripped from the computer. The professor slid down the wall and took off the earphones.

"That's Akihide Kubo. We got him. The connection is the phone. Tell Les to keep his phone on next time."

"Yes professor."

The plastic netting cast with an easy motion over the strawberry patch. The surrounding weeds, young and tender, let go of the soil with a little tug from Les. The task was done in under an hour so he went to the door and knocked but no one answered.

"Oh well," Les said as he shrugged and went down to the garage to pick up his roller blades.

Only half the day was done and the rest of the afternoon was his to do as he wished. He wondered how he was going to meet Rachel and decided to tell P.J. the story. Les wasn't sure if P.J. would think he was crazy and that scared him but he needed his help. He was good at planning. The roller blades slipped on and down the even streets Les went. The groomed campus of Upton College passed by on his way home under the strong summer sky.

Chapter 11: A reveal.

A stream of frothy water carrying soap suds down to the street flowed from P.J.'s driveway where he was washing his Jeep. Les rolled right through and left a wet trail behind as he came to a stop behind P.J. who wasn't looking at anything but the door in front of him that was covered in mud and chunks of sod from a recent off-road adventure. In P.J.'s hand, a sponge dripped soapy drops down to the shadow growing below his feet. He flipped his sunglasses up onto the top of his head and spun around. There, Les was standing with a smear of mud across his face and his shoes in hand.

"Dude, you got some schmutz on your face," P.J. said.

Les rolled up to the side mirror and leaned in. His eyes closed for a second.

"Shit, had this on me the whole time," Les said.

"Hey watch the swearing. They might think it's me. My father has bugs planted I think. Well that's what he said and I wouldn't put it past him," P.J. said.

"That's right. You've got that no swearing for a trip deal. So excuse me, anyone who is listening, I said shit and not P.J.," Les said with a smile and wiped his face off with his forearm.

"You're just trying to take my last nerve ain't ya boy? And hate to say it but even wiping the dirt off your face isn't going to help ya," P.J. said.

"Funny. Speaking of funny, I was skating down Verna Hill and a convertible Beamer rolled by with a flock of college girls. They all looked at me and giggled. Now I know why," Les said.

"You and the college girl thing. You realize when you get there that the girls aren't magically different. Same old scene but with more freedom," P.J. said.

He picked up the hose while Les nodded. P.J. squeezed the gun like handle and sprayed the Jeep clean. The last of the soap and water dripped to the driveway and joined the stream of water heading out to the street.

"Dude, can we talk. I need your help," Les asked.

"Sure bro. Sling it," P.J. said.

"Cool. This is going to be a little weird so let me take off these blades. I think we need to sit," Les said.

P.J.'s left eyebrow lifted.

"Okay, let me turn off the hose and we can kibbutz on the deck. Don't worry. Mother won't bother us. She's at a tennis lesson."

Les noticed his hand begin to shake a bit as they sat on the porch under the columns of shade. The dry air cooled his hands but his palms began to sweat anyway. P.J. poured into a chair and crossed his ankles. The cushion under Les was hard with wear so he shimmied back and forth trying to get comfortable as he scratched his knees. The wide sunglasses on P.J.'s head rotated down over his eyes with a tug.

"Had to put these on since you sound so serious. Got to get into ninja mode," P.J. said.

"What ever bro. Don't even know why I'm telling you this," Les said and puffed his cheeks with a slow exhale.

"Spit it out dork. What could you say that would freak me out? Nada," P.J. said and sat up straight.

"Been talking to Aki and he wants me to help the girl who got his liver," Les said.

"I stand corrected. What?"

"I've been talking to Aki on my cell phone. He called me but there are limited minutes," Les said.

"Wow! Even in the afterlife, the phone companies screw you," P.J. said.

"Funny. I'm serious dude. No BS. Clear as day and even went to Eddie's aunt for help," Les said and sat back.

"You are serious. What did Aki say?"

"Said a girl Rachel who lives in Clover isn't moving on with her life so he can't go to the bright side. He said I have to help," Les said.

"Can I talk to him on the phone?"

"I called him once but he said not to call him and he will call me because of the time and shit," Les said.

"Dude, swearing."

"Sorry. Didn't even know Aki was a donor but he named the girl and I googled her. She had a transplant. You think I'm crazy?" Les asked.

"Entirely, but I believe you. I saw my grandfather after he died," P.J. said and took off his sunglasses.

"Really?"

"Yeah dude, he said I'd be all right and not to worry about him. Changed everything. Wasn't afraid to talk to my rents about anything after that," P.J. said.

"Did you know Aki was a donor?"

"No, but you know his parents. They weren't going to say anything. You know I never got to say goodbye to them before they moved. You?" P.J. asked.

"Nope. So, will you help me find this girl?" Les asked.

"How could I not bro? Got to help Aki," P.J. said.

"Thanks," Les said and turned to shield his face from his friend as he pretended to itch his nose but really wiped away a tear.

"I miss him too," P.J. said.

A male silence sat between them. The sounds of cars passing by invaded their quiet moment.

"Okay. Here's how I see it. We find her. We get you to talk to her, probably be the biggest problem, and then we take her to have some fun. You know, show her life is worth living. So how old is she?" P.J. asked.

"Think she's a senior or was. Don't know if she graduated or not."

"I know a guy Jameson from Clover high who might help. I'm his instructor," P.J. said.

"At…?"

"Jujitsu you dumb… dummy. Almost got me there. Come on let's go inside and see what we can find online," P.J. said.

"Already tried," Les said.

"You tried. I didn't. Let's go."

Up in P.J.'s room, a room where the bed was always made and clothes never touch the floor, they fired up P.J's over-powered laptop at his orderly desk and went online. Three searches were run but uncovered nothing more than before. Emails were checked and then P.J. sent a message to Jameson asking if he knew Rachel.

"Yo, can you go onto Craigslist?" Les asked.

"Why? Nothing but pervs," P.J. said.

"They do sell stuff you know. Just wanted to check the free stuff to see if anyone was getting rid of a drafting table," Les said.

"Fine."

The site came up and right to the section for free things they went but no drafting tables were listed.

"All junk bro, want to go on the personals?" P.J. asked.

"Figures and no. See if that Jameson dude got back to you."

Jameson had not replied and so Les compelled P.J. to watch a trailer for a new Ubisoft game on a free gaming site he found through lifehack.org. On the website, Les saw that they were selling The Star Wars: The Force Unleashed Two and The Old Republic MMO for cheap and he got excited.

"Yo, couldn't afford those games before but now I have some cash. Awesome. With the money from this gig, I'll grab a new deck and the games in one shot," Les said.

"What happened to your old deck?"

"Busted."

"Beat."

"Yeah ."

"But I thought you were saving for that new scintillator art stuff or something?" P.J. asked.

"It's Cintiq. Don't know if I'm going that route anymore. Reckless expensive too."

"Like?" P.J. asked.

"Like a strikeout."

"Over a K?"

"True. Over a grand."

"Beat."

"Beat down. So really don't think I'm crazy?" Les asked.

"No, I said I thought you were entirely crazy but I believe you, which makes me crazy."

"Guess so," Les said and P.J. got up from his chair and walked over to his bookshelf.

"Just had a thought," he said and pulled out a phone book.

"What you doing?" Les asked.

"It's a phone book. What's the girl's last name again?"

"Higgs."

The phonebook spread open and nimble fingers went through the yellow pages over to the white ones. P.J.'s finger landed on a name. He carried the book over and plopped it on the desk.

"There's only one Higgs in Clover. We typed in too much info. Skewed our search. Higgs 309 Rowland Road," P.J. said.

"Leave it to you to go all primitive on me even though you got the best tech."

"Worked. Okay L, that's where we start. You should drive by her house see what's up. Don't be all stalker and sit there. Just drive by and then go to any local stores where you might find people our age and ask around. Say you met her at camp when you were kids or something and knew she lived there," P.J. said, sat and went to check his emails.

"I was thinking maybe I could say, like, I was doing research on transplants for my college essay and wanted to talk to her," Les said.

"That's awesome. Use that. That way you eliminate the creep factor," P.J. said and deleted a few Spam emails.

"Uh, one problem. I can't get there. Will you drive me? I don't want to ask Eddie to help me again. She's done enough."

"I'm pretty busy this week man. But... I'll drive you there once. You need to start driving again dude but I get it," P.J. said.

"I know. Just not now."

"Fine. We will go tomorrow around ten," P.J. said.

"I have to go to my gig first."

"Oh you didn't tell me about that yet. So?" P.J. asked.

"Crazy professor paying me bills to fill out forms and take some tests in a study."

"Cool. Like drugs?"

"No, I don't think so. Think it's just some brain study. Brain development or something. Just started," Les said.

"Then we'll have to go around two. Oh what'd ya know? Jameson," P.J. said.

He read the message. He shrugged. He closed the laptop.

"He knows who she is but isn't friends. Said she lived on Rowland by his bud," P.J. said.

"This is going to suck."

"Dude, suck it up. The rents will be here soon and I have to go put air in the tires. Want a ride?" P.J. asked.

"Nah, I'll skate."

"Cool."

Wind picked up and jumped from treetop to treetop as Les skated down the even streets. Crows cawed and flocked in front of his house as he glided into the open garage where his father was covering the front end of the Fiat with what he called a bra.

"Good day at work?" Mr. Logan asked.

"Not bad," Les said and he sat on the step to the door leading inside.

He placed the roller blades next to the stairs.

"So anything you want to tell me?" Mr. Logan asked.

"No, but why are you home so early?" Les asked.

"Took some work home," Mr. Logan said.

"You always take work home," Les said.

"This time a little more," Mr. Logan said.

"Sucks."

"Yes it does Les. I'd watch out inside. I think Wooly is on the prowl for you."

"Right. Got to shower now. I stink a ton," Les said.

As he stepped inside the door to the house, Wooly Bully bound upon him. To the floor they fell, and Les got a good tongue lashing for leaving Wooly Bully behind for the day. Mr. Logan laughed and said to himself, "Boy got a good sweat from work." His eyes fogged up a touch with tears of pride as he nodded his head.

Wooly Bully sat outside the bathroom door as Les showered and followed him into his room as Les left a series of wet footprints behind. Wooly Bully pounced onto the bed and rubbed his nose and stretched out. The piles of clothes on the floor were getting higher, high enough to put books on, and Les couldn't find anything that wasn't too stiff until he remembered to look under the bed. There a pack of new white t-shirts sat unopened and next to them his favorite red O'Neal board shorts.

Feeling refreshed and clad in a new soft shirt, he pet Wooly Bully and headed over to his computer. A web site on ghosts and the afterlife was pulled up. Les's door swung open and startled him as it crashed into a pile of clothes. Nothing was there so he turned back around.

"Must be Aki, Wooly," Les said.

"What?"

"Holy, you scared me Dad," Les said as he turned to see his father.

"Sorry, just telling you dinner will be early."

"Okay. Uh, Dad, can I use one of your cards to get a new game for the Playstation? I'll give you the cash when the professor pays me," Les said.

"Sure, I'll give you the numbers after dinner. Proud of you kid," Mr. Logan said.

"Thanks."

The blunt footsteps of Mr. Logan bound down the hall until they faded at the stairs. Les closed his door and heard his phone buzz on his nightstand. Aki's number came up.

"Hey, I found her," Les said.

"I know. Thanks. I don't have much time. Listen. Be careful around the professor," Aki said.

"How did you know?"

"I felt the phone go to the other side of town so I followed it," Aki said.

"Can you like watch me anytime?" Les asked.

"No, not really. I'm not God L. I'm just dead. Can't explain but be careful. Time is running out," Aki said.

"Okay I will. Dude's a scruff. I could take him if I had to."

"Uh, no you couldn't. Not important. L you have to get to Rachel soon. I feel things falling apart. By the way, you should get the new drawing tablet and software. Not the games. Trust me. Gotta bounce. I'll call soon."

The dial tone filled Les's ear.

Chapter 12: Over hill, over dale.

The next morning came like a rider on the horse of night. In the sky, a thin overcast spread silver light over New Hebron. On Brookside Lane, Professor Gluck went over Les's data. Lazlo synced up the audio recording and the video at the computer. Professor Gluck stood above the corner desk palms flat on the surface as he rifled through the dry pages. One page grabbed his attention. He read it over and over again. His flat palms became fists and pounded on the desk as his eye twitched. Lazlo spun in his chair and looked at the professor who had his eyes closed and was taking deep breaths.

"What's wrong?" Lazlo asked.

"Les is an artist and scored high on the temporal lobe sensitivity scale."

"Oh, not good. That would make him prone to magnetic field induced sensations and coupled with an imaginative mind might make this all wrong. He might just been seeing things," Lazlo said.

"That's exactly what experimental psychologists and my colleagues would say. You read about what they did to Doctor Persinger after the Swedes had problems replicating his test results. What we're doing is too important to be invalidated by a corrupted subject. But we do have the audio."

"Going to look and listen again in a second. Speaking of Persinger, we're using the God helmet today right? I set it up and the room should be shielded from EM fields," Lazlo said.

"Yes, we are. I just hope he doesn't see god."

"That would be bad," Lazlo said.

The door bell rang.

"It's him. We need to up the sensitivity on the instruments. Go over the recording again. I'll be back," Professor Gluck said.

Down the hardwood stairs, white lab coat flapping across the banister, Professor Gluck missed the last step and came to a hard halt. He stopped, straightened his coat, put on a large smile, and opened the door.

Les stood there with a tuft of hair standing straight up like an angry cockatoo from skating over so quickly after his shower. The professor waved him in.

"Hey professor," Les said.

"Good day. Please follow me downstairs. I have a fun experiment for you," Professor Gluck said.

Down in the basement, Les placed his roller blades in Cell-17 and then walked behind the professor to a room down the hall. A desk with a computer and monitor sat outside the painted cinderblock wall. Les smelled mildew and thought the dampness wasn't good for electronics.

"So today we are going to start with a perception test," Professor Gluck said.

"Cool. Like what?"

"You are going to put on a helmet that uses solenoids to create complex but weak magnetic fields and we are going to see what you see or feel. Not dangerous at all, the magnetic fields are weaker than what your microwave puts out but they will be focused on the temporal lobe of your brain," Professor Gluck said.

"Sound kind of science fictiony. Everyone does this?"

"Oh yes. Many quite enjoy the experience."

"What's that?"

"Now if I told you it might alter the results. The brain is a powerful thing.

"All right," Les said

"Behind that door is a recliner, please sit and get comfortable. We will put the helmet on you and then induce a weak magnetic field. You will be blindfolded and I will need any electronic devices you have. They might influence the fields," Professor Gluck said.

"Well…"

"I have your money by the way Les," Professor Gluck said lifted his hand towards the doorknob.

"Cool."

Les's face brightened and he brushed the tuft of hair flat with his hand.

"I'll set you up and then Lazlo will get you in an hour after the experiment is done. When you are done, please fill out the survey on the table next to the recliner."

"Cool."

Inside the small windowless chamber sat an out-of-place plush brown recliner. Les could tell it was an old laundry room from the sealed up clothes shoot in the ceiling and the lingering scent of dried detergent. He piled into the seat and it accepted him with a squeal. The professor got the God helmet off of a fold out table in the corner.

"That looks like an ancient motorcycle helmet," Les said.

"Actually it's a snowmobile helmet and is a perfect replica of the Koren helmet designed by Stanley Koren. Don't worry about the wires, they don't get hot or anything. The blindfold is on the table next to the survey," Professor Gluck said.

A sleeping mask Les had seen in movies but never in real life laid flat on the table. He slipped on the blindfold and it was more comfy than he expected. The professor placed the white helmet with multicolored wires streaming from the sides gently over Les's head.

"I know it looks crazy with all of those little metal connectors and wires. How does it feel?" Professor Gluck asked.

Les could hear just enough to make out the question. He gave the professor a thumbs up but felt like a dork doing so.

"Very good. Just relax and take it all in. Don't force anything and just remember what happens," Professor Gluck said.

Les once gain gave the thumbs up with a cringe on his face. The helmet was powered up and lights shut off. The professor exited with Les's phone in hand.

At the end of the testing rooms, Lazlo held onto the banister of the stairs and then saw the phone in Professor Gluck's hand. His eyes widened and he rushed to the professor with his hand outstretched.

"That the unit?" Lazlo asked.

"The only phone he had on him."

"May I?" Lazlo asked.

The professor handed him the phone. Lazlo's eyes went even wider as he inspected the phone's contents.

"So?"

"No stored numbers or recent calls from Akihide Kubo but I can set it up so we can access his voice mail and track him if we call him and he answers," Lazlo said.

"Do it," Professor Gluck said.

The darkness felt heavy on Les's legs. His knees itched and burned with pricks of heat. Glimmers of fire flickered around the corners of his eyes. Then, the heaviness began to lift off of Les, or so he thought, and he felt the chair fall away from his body.

"This is reckless filthy. Holy crap. Can't feel my legs."

Les swayed back and forth as he felt like he was tumbling inside an ocean wave. The fires in the corners of his eyes extinguished and left wisps of smoke behind that circulated to the front of the darkness. There was no fear in Les. No anxiety itched at his knees. Then all went still.

"This is kind of awesome," Les said and felt pressure build around him.

In Les's mind, the wisps of smoke collected around him, above him, and expanded into human form but no faces appeared.

"Aki dude, that you?" Les asks.

No reply came but the sensation of taking off in a plane pinned him to the back of the recliner.

"Whoa, this is getting freaky."

A tickle of calm rippled down his arms, across his chest, and ran in streams down to his toes where it fizzled. Les couldn't help but chuckle. He'd been ticklish since he could remember. The darkness lightened to a twilight stretched airy thin to the corners of his perception and he could feel his body again.

"Awesome. Oh, wait a second," Les said.

The fires in the corners of his eyes returned and grew to roaring flames that encircled him. Les could not feel the heat but he felt anger emitted from the blaze as it scaled the emptiness above him. Three thuds pounded through him. The fires dissolved and Les realized the noises were knocks. He felt a hand.

The blindfold lifted and allowed in the painful light. Les saw Lazlo standing before him with one eyebrow up and his mouth crimped with a sour expression. Lazlo motioned to take off the helmet. Les nodded yes and the Koren helmet, the God helmet, tugged on his ears as it slid off.

"Weird huh?" Lazlo asked as he placed the helmet on the corner table.

"Yup."

"While the experience is fresh in you memory, write a brief description on blank paper and answer the survey. I'll be back in twenty to get the info," Lazlo said.

"That didn't seem like an hour," Les said.

"Everyone experiences time differently with the experiment. For some it seems much longer and for others much shorter."

Lazlo left, leaving the door wide open, and Les jotted down his experience and answered the survey. From the questions Les could tell his experience wasn't unique. The only thing that bothered him was that he didn't know what time it really was.

As Les's pencil hit the table, Lazlo and the professor came through the door. There was little room to breathe.

"That was sort of fun professor," Les said.

"I'm glad. Some people don't experience anything," Professor Gluck said and motioned for Lazlo to get the survey. He did and left.

"Could I have my phone now?" Les asked.

"Of course," Professor Gluck said and pulled it out of his lab coat's pocket.

"Thanks," Les said, looked at the time, and continued, "I have to go. Didn't think that much time went by. Hate to rush you but can I have the money?"

"Of course. It's right here," Professor Gluck said.

He handed Les an envelope from his other coat pocket.

"Is there anything else?" Les asked.

"Not today. But if you happen to see or hear anything unusual, please call me. It might be from the temporal lobe stimulation and is important to the study. And I do mean anything, from voices to deja vous," Professor Gluck said.

"Okay, I will. Bye," Les said.

"How about you come by Friday morning, not tomorrow, for another evaluation?"

"Okay professor," Les said as he breeched the doorway.

"Also," Professor Gluck said, Les stopped and looked back, "you did a great job with the strawberries. You can cut the lawn on Monday okay?"

"Okay. Thanks. See you later."

Down the even streets, Les raced home. It was one o'clock and P.J. wanted to leave at two. Through town he dodged lunchtime traffic, weaving through stacks of cars and delivery trucks. Energy flowed through Les. He hadn't felt this strong since before he broke his leg. Les skated as hard as he could and gained speed down hill as he flew by cars. The world became a blur as he broke the speed limit and could only hear the rush of air.

Les turned the corner onto his road, kids played street hockey a few houses down, and P.J.'s Jeep was in the driveway. He felt his phone vibrate in his pocket and pulled it out to look. As he lifted the phone up to see, he hit the curb and tumbled across his lawn. Les never dropped the phone and as he got up he saw that his elbows and knees were stained green from the lawn. In the driver's seat, P.J. clapped and shook his head.

"Nice landing. I give it an eleven," P.J. said.

Wooly Bully barked at the window. Les showed P.J. the phone so he'd know he was distracted. Les answered.

"Hello," Les said and rubbed a clump of dirt off his elbow.

"Hi Les, this is Professor Gluck. Just wanted to remind you that if you see anything unusual please let me know, and also, bring lunch on Friday. It might be a long session."

"Oh. Okay professor."

"Very good. Good bye Les."

"Bye."

In the professor's second story computer room, he hung up the phone and looked at Lazlo.

"You get it?" he asked.

"He's at home. The track works."

Chapter 13: Throwing down.

Clover wasn't far from New Hebron. A few exits on the interstate, a few miles of tree lined roads, and they were there. The Jeep rolled off the exit and through a few traffic lights that P.J. didn't think needed to be there. Clover had the same layout as New Hebron but without the college and on a smaller scale making it easier to navigate, especially with the dashboard GPS telling them where to go. The rush of air through the open Jeep impeded P.J. and Les from talking, so they yelled.

"I like the older GPS units with the English accent," P.J. said with hands at ten and two on the steering wheel.

"That was like years ago when they came out in Beamers and Benzes," Les said and watched a beetle splat into the windshield.

"Yeah my dad's first seven series had one," P.J. said and jammed on the brakes at a four way stop.

An elderly lady with a cane and a plastic shopping bag scowled at them from the sidewalk. Les waved for her to go on. She denied his courtesy with a swat of her hand. P.J. hit the gas and after a half-mile they turned down a flat elm lined street named Sycamore Way.

"That old lady almost makes me want to swear. I'm all nice to her and what?" P.J. asked and shook his head.

"She probably thought you would run her over. I would," Les said.

P.J. flashed a glance and took his right hand off the steering wheel. In between the seats, a clear message was given.

"Dude, you're not supposed to swear," Les said.

"This is a gesture, not a word," P.J. said and took a right like the GSP told him.

"Now that I can hear, can we flip on the tunes?" Les asked.

"Sure but you're not going to like what I have in the iPod," P.J. said and took a left like the GPS told him.

"Why? You still doing music research? You're onto the eighties noise now aren't you?"

"Yes, FYI, Psychedelic Furs and New Order are awesome. Everything you listen to now comes from New Wave in the eighties anyway. Might as well go to the source," P.J. said.

They slowed to a stop at a crosswalk to allow kids and their parents to cross the street from the daycare in a large brick church.

"Mastodon and Death Angel don't sound anything like eighties music," Les said.

"Ugh, really, you're listening to that? Just tell me you won't grow your hair out stalker long," P.J. said.

"Not promising anything, but I like The All-American Rejects, Automatic Love Letter and Polar Bear club too," Les said and smacked his friend's shoulder.

They arrived at the Higgs' household, or so that's what the GPS said. No one was outside the yellow house with a hedge framed yard on 309 Rowland Road. They stopped for a second as the engine rumbled and churned. The foot met the pedal and they rolled away.

Rowland led to a grassy entrance to a squat town park that was bordered with a crisscrossed log fence where a pond called Perry's spread for hundreds of yards. The pebble strewn banks on the other side of the lake were surrounded by a forest. It reminded Les of the Cascades. They came to a stop at the entrance. Les looked over the hump of grass and saw a small rock beach below where a couple of boys with freckled arms were catching Sunnies on makeshift fishing rods.

"So, we know where she lives. And what else do we know?" P.J. asked.

"I know where she worked. She worked at Carvel's," Les said.

"Dope coincidence, I was in the mood for some soft serve. That's where we'll make a connection. Where's the Carvel?"

"Uh, here in Clover I guess."

"I see. Look it up."

"I can't."

"Why?"

"My phone doesn't do that."

"Oh forgot you have that cell you need to crank. Gah."

The latest version of the iPhone slipped out of P.J.'s pocket like it wanted to breathe. He tapped the screen. He expanded the screen. He googled. He found out where the closest Carvel was situated.

A breeze kicked up the scent of fresh water over the Jeep and Les could taste the moisture on his tongue. A bouquet of lavender, primrose and pine mixed to blanket a soft perfume across the banks of Perry's Pond. Les saw a man up the street walking a golden retriever and he thought of Wooly Bully. P.J. set in the coordinates

"Okay Cookie Puss, here we come," P.J. said.

"What the…?"

"Cookie Puss. The ice cream cake. You haven't seen the Carvel commercials from like a decade ago? They're on Youtube. Tres goof," P.J. said.

"Cool. Hopefully we'll be in luck," Les said.

P.J. put his phone back into his pocket and fished out a quarter with a whole in the center. It caught the sun and reflected in Les's face. He put up his hand to shield himself and P.J. lowered the coin.

"It's my lucky quarter. Found it the day I decided to not be afraid anymore and take up MMA. It was the day after I saw my grandfather. Ever since, things have worked out and you get to borrow it. Borrow it, not keep," P.J. said and flicked the coin. Les snagged it out of the air and a half smile grew.

"Thanks bro."

The GPS took them on an out of the way route and when they reached the strip mall where Carvel was wedged between a nail salon and a Radio Shack they discovered a sign on the door that read "Closed for Renovations".

They parked and P.J. shut off the engine. The traffic passed by and cut through the air with high to low tones.

"Not good," Les said.

"Beat, totally, but just a minor set back. Now we go where she would hang. Luckily I emailed Jameson that very question last night and I have a list."

"Maybe I should just call her and tell her everything?" Les asked.

"That would make you look rubber room ready bro. I know what we're doing now is a bit odd but it will pay off if we do our homework. Who knows? You might meet someone," P.J. said.

"Fine, let's bounce. Where to?" Les asked.

"Where else? Starbucks."

The Jeep tore off and spit asphalt as the tires ground up the road. Off into the day of sapphire blue skies they went, air flowing over them and sun shining down like a spotlight tracking their every move. They didn't need the GPS to find Starbucks. It's always downtown.

Les and P.J. could smell the coffee from a half mile away and followed the scent by a four story brick office building to the corner. Starbucks stabbed out at a cross roads with a white façade like a pimple on the buildings behind. They found an open space in the lot and soon found out why. A dumpster of coffee shop garbage abuzz with flies and bulging with plastic bags was right in front of them.

The pops and hisses from the espresso machines, steamers on full, and coffee makers reverberated off Les and P.J. as they entered the store. A dense atmosphere highlighted with the aroma of ground beans and whipped cream greeted them.

They stood in line and P.J. nudged Les's arm.

"What?" Les asked.

"Say it."

"Say what?"

"The comment you always say when we go to Starbucks."

"Don't follow."

"About your dream girl."

"You mean Starbuck?"

"Yes."

"Dude, after watching the whole of BSG, Battlestar Galactica, again I've moved on from Kara Thrace AKA Starbuck. More of Boomer man now."

"I have no idea what that means, but how things change. I thought you'd make the Starbuck comment and there you go and surprise me."

"Want me to say it?"

"Not if you don't mean it."

"Okay. Damn. This place looks just like the one in South Stanford we went to after the Fallout Boy concert," Les said.

"Does have the same layout. So, you going to Nerdi Gras in October?" P.J. asked.

"For one, Nerdi Gras is in San Diego in July, but you're asking about the one in New York right?" Les asked.

P.J. nodded.

"No, I don't think I'm going to the con in NYC," Les said.

"But you and Aki talked about it forever after you missed the last one," P.J. said.

"It just doesn't seem important."

The line moved but stalled again when an older customer asked for a large coffee and the barista had to explain their ordering system. Shrugs and eye rolls ran rampant through the patrons. Les listened to a pair of over-caffeinated soccer moms talk about how happy they were that a Whole Foods was going in the abandoned industrial complex on the other side of town. Orders were placed and they waited to go mingle.

Lattes in hand, the two went outside. They wandered over to a small patch of grass by the road where a patio was set up surrounded by a terraced flower garden with three umbrellas, three tables, and crosshatched metal bench. All were set in the blazing sun and all were occupied by bodies large and small. A square of shade from a green awning by a side door provided the only shelter so they took it. Four guys with tight cropped haircuts and even tighter t-shirts puffed up in their seats and examined the trespassers of their domain.

"Les, think those dudes are eyeing us. Let it slide," P.J. said.

"Great."

A pair of girls in flowery tops and jean shorts turned the corner and then looked back toward the Jeep. One girl sipped on her Chai ice tea as she looked over the crowd. The other pulled out the straw from her cup, sucked the ice coffee off the bottom, and placed it back in. P.J. leaned to Les.

"Perfect. One wink and they'll come over," P.J. said and winked a quick wink.

The girls with suburban symmetry spotted P.J.'s invitation and step in step they walked over with a swing to their hips. Les couldn't feel his pulse when they stopped almost nose to nose with them.

"Lovely day ladies," P.J. said.

"Hi, I'm Mandy," the tea drinker said.

"I'm Veronica," the iced coffee drinker said.

"I'm P.J. and this is L."

"Three letters between you. How mysterious," Veronica said.

"We know everyone around here and every car. That's your Jeep right? Adorb. You're not from around here?" Mandy asked in a flurry.

"Yes it is and no we're not. We're from New Hebron," P.J. said.

The guys with the tight t-shirts got up. P.J. took off his sunglasses. The guys walked by and tossed their take out coffee cups in the trash on the sidewalk. Les was relieved.

"Tools," Mandy said.

"They think they're Russian mafia or something lame," Veronica said.

"Then we won't let them in our fun. So, let's sit, tell me about yourself," P.J. said and escorted them to the empty table.

P.J. dazzled the girls with wit and quotes from Voltaire he'd memorized. Les let P.J. spin the stories but came to realize that P.J. was getting distracted so he decided to jump in.

"Uh, Mandy, you said you know everyone around here. Do you know Rachel Higgs?" Les asked.

"Sure, Rachel's awesome, not conceited like so many other girls, but she got sick and left school for months like she had Mono or something. She bailed on graduation. I think she just has to take the exams though. How do you know her?" Mandy asked.

"I'm doing my college essay on organ donation and read about her in a newspaper article online when I was doing research," Les said.

"Cool, where you applying? I'm applying to Colgate but my safety school is UConn," Veronica said.

"Cool, I'm applied to five schools. Mostly state U's. Hey, wondering, do you know where Rachel hangs out? I'd like to talk to her about what happened," Les said.

"She doesn't go out anymore. Haven't seen her in months," Mandy said.

"Really," P.J. said.

"Really. I heard her parents were strict before but when she got sick they went all hyper-paranoid. She's like a bubble girl," Mandy said.

"Yeah, totally sheltered," Veronica said.

"That sucks. Won't be able to contact her, there goes my essay," Les said.

"Want her email addy? She's cool and will probably help you," Mandy said.

"That would be great," Les said and with that P.J. pulled out his phone anticipating that the girls might react poorly to Les's ancient device.

"What is it darling?" P.J. asked.

Mandy spelled out the address while curious sounds of squeaking metal coils came from around the other side of the store.

"Thanks so much. Hey. What is that?" Les said, stood up and went to investigate.

In the Jeep sat two of the guys with tight t-shirts and on the hood sat the others. Les's head sank. The last thing he wanted was trouble but he had to tell P.J.

"Bro, the Jeep. Trouble. Those dudes."

"Excuse me," P.J. said to the girls.

The girls looked at each other and Mandy had her phone in her hand. An itch grew on Les's knees but he didn't scratch. P.J. and Les walked the corner and P.J. put his hands up in front of him and shook his head with a smile.

"Gentlemen, I think you've mistaken my ride for someone else's. So if you wouldn't mind, please don't scratch the leather while getting out. Thanks," P.J. said and Les brought his hands to his waist.

The two on the hood hopped off. One with a glaring diamond earring led the way and they stepped up to Les and P.J. who tilted his head to the side and looked the guys up and down.

"Thanks. And you two in the seats, if you wouldn't mind," P.J. said and stood straight.

"Mind what? You should mind ya business boy," the earring guy said.

"That is my business and I think we're about the same age so…"

"So what? Huh?"

"So get out of my face," P.J. said.

"We're leaving so why don't you just let us," Les said.

"Asking permission. Good, you should. You know who we are?" the earring guy asked. The two others hopped out of the Jeep.

"No idea, so…" Les said.

"We're the players around here," he said and P.J. couldn't stop himself. Muffled chuckles escaped.

"What you laughing at boy," said the guy who was sitting in the driver seat.

"Too much to explain but thanks for getting out of my Jeep," P.J. said.

Les stepped in front of P.J knowing all too well what he could do.

"We're going to take off. No need to get serious," Les said.

"Good. Listen to your boyfriend there and bounce boy," the earring guy said.

"Sorry Les… You see he's not my boyfriend. But you're cute," P.J. said.

"You're a queer," the earring guy said.

"You know that's our word, boy."

Les's right foot stepped back to secure his footing as the guys rushed them. The guy with the earring threw a wide right hook at P.J. and to P.J.'s eyes it must have been in slow motion. He stepped into the guy's body with a twist to evade the punch and as his back hit the earring guy's chest, P.J. grabbed his arm and flipped him to the ground. Les never saw the punch that knocked him down.

Two guys attacked P.J and another Les. Les got his hand up and blocked a few kicks from the ground and then pounced up. The hockey instincts, long dormant, awoke and Les popped his opponent in the nose and grabbed his tight t-shirt and dragged it over the guy's head.

P.J. dodged two other attackers like they were ten year old boys trying to fight their father. Jabs and elbows crushed their teenage faces. Then, the earring guy got up and charged P.J. who sent him back to the ground with a front kick to the stomach. The guy who was sitting in the driver's seat swung at P.J who grabbed hold of his arm and twisted it like taffy until he screamed. Les threw a few heavy rights that mostly grazed his opponent's head as he tore the tight t-shirt off from around the guy's head. The young hoods, who dreamt of being tough and terrifying, fled around the corner bloody and whimpering. A flash of blue and red caught Les attention from down the street. The cops were coming.

Chapter 14: Busted.

At the Clover police department, Les and P.J. sat in a locked room with a transparent door known as the Hold. The clean cell was mostly used for drunks who got rowdy late at night. Fortunately, it was still late afternoon.

"You're going to call your parent's now?" Les asked.

"Yup, it will be nasty when I get home. But don't worry, they won't make a scene with you around," P.J. said.

A gray haired sergeant, square and stout, stepped in front of the door and unlocked it with a round of jingling keys.

"Come on. The girls that called had a video too. You're clear. You were just defending yourself," the sergeant said.

"No charges?" P.J. asked.

"No charges but you could press some. The others are in a cell around the corner."

Les looked at P.J. and P.J. looked at Les. They shrugged together.

"No," Les said.

"Sure?" asked the sergeant.

"Yes, unless they're dangerous and you need us to," P.J. said.

"No, just some young men who haven't figured out who they are yet," the sergeant said.

They were led down the hall by a clerk's office and out to the front where a row of benches nestled along the wall. Metal loops for handcuffs were drilled into the cinder block walls above the seats. P.J. sat and Les stood as the officer took a deep sigh and blinked twice.

"You're in the system here and so I'd advise that you don't come back to Clover for awhile. Can't have any more incidents. We'll be on the lookout for you. But you're in luck, we decided not to impound your Jeep. You can leave after you sign a form," he said.

"Great," P.J. said.

"I'll get you your things," the sergeant said.

Outside, a few minutes later on the stone steps, P.J. called his parents and explained the situation because he thought if the cops called his parents first then the trouble would be worse. As he hung up, he pointed to a dark puffy bruise on Les's cheek bone that had snuck up below his eye.

"That hurt?" P.J. asked.

"It's sore but not too bad. Think I'll get a shiner?" Les asked.

"Yup. Do already. Listen bro, sorry to say I won't be able to see you for a while. I'm under lock and key for a couple weeks."

"You mean you're grounded?" Les asked.

"Like a lightning rod. You'll have to contact Rachel without me."

"How am I going to get here?"

"Don't know bro but Aki chose you to help him. I'm out for now," P.J. said.

The ride home was filled with the songs of New Order. Les didn't care for them at all. With a turn off the highway and a stretch of even road, the Jeep pulled in front of Les's house, a house guarded by trees, a house simple as the white paint on the sides. Wooly Bully howled from inside. The friends shook hands and a wave sent P.J off to deal with his ordeal. Les was alone now and didn't know what he was going to do.

Wooly Bully was a tornado of tail and tongue as Les walked in the door. Any attempt to make a subtle entry was lost. His mother called to him and he went to the kitchen where he saw a plate covered in plastic wrap on the counter. Mrs. Logan tried to talk but Wooly Bully's happy whimpers and hard panting got in the way. Les knelt down to pet the dog and Wooly Bully plopped down to roll on his back. He rubbed Wooly Bully's tummy and looked up to his mother. Her eyes narrowed with confusion as she examined his face and then they expanded with concern.

"What happened to your face?" she asked.

"Roller blade accident. Missed a grind," Les said.

"Oh, does it still hurt?"

"No, it's fine. See," Les said and pressed the red spot on his cheek bone.

"Okay, chicken kebabs and curry vegetables are waiting for you," she said.

Les found it curious that his father wasn't commenting from the other room.

"Where's Dad?"

"Garage. You. Eat."

So Les ate standing at the counter, secretly tossing bits of chicken down to Wooly Bully, breaking the prohibition on people food, and waited for his father to come in but he didn't. After the plate was cleaned off and stowed in the dishwasher Les made his way to the garage.

"Hey Dad. What you doing?" Les said from the doorway.

"Hey Les, what happened? Get in a fight?"

Les looked over his shoulder into the house, closed the door behind him, and walked over to his father.

"Actually, yeah, I did but don't tell Mom. You know how she got when I had the hockey fights," Les said.

"Yes I do. You all right? Come here," Mr. Logan said.

Les got closer and Mr. Logan pressed his finger on three spots along his eye socket.

"Pain?" he asked.

"Nope."

"You're good then. So, plead your case," Mr. Logan said.

"P.J. and I went to Clover…"

"Clover? Why did you go there?"

"No big deal Dad, P.J. and I just wanted to go meet new people."

"Sounds like you did. Go on."

"So we went to Starbuck, some dudes who thought they were a gang or something eyeballed us when we sat outside and talked to some girls…"

"Pretty?"

"Okay."

"Okay? You and P.J. should be hitting on hot chicks."

"Dad, please don't say hot chicks."

Les rolled his eyes. Mr. Logan wiped his hands with a rag from a workbench.

"Okay. Go on."

"The chumps went and sat in P.J.'s Jeep. Two sat on the hood too. Asked them to get out and leave but they stepped up and swung. That's it," Les said and stepped back.

"Young men being territorial and stupid sounds about right. If they swung first then all you could do was defend yourself. But, what do I always say about violence?"

"Men settle disputes with their minds and animals do with their claws."

"Glad you remembered. Anything else?" Mr. Logan asked and a smile rose.

"Yeah, the cops picked us up but…"

"I know. Glad you didn't lie to me," Mr. Logan said.

"Dad, why have you been out here for like a half an hour?"

"Thinking about selling the Fiat."

"Why?"

"Cost too much in insurance and taxes not to be driven. We could save a good amount of money if I took it off our policy. I was hoping you would be manning the helm by now."

"You know I haven't driven since the accident."

"Start now. You'll have more freedom. And, it will help out your mother and me. I saved the Fiat because I wanted you to have a cool car in high school. I had a clunker."

"I suck at driving stick."

"I know. Let's practice."

"Now?"

"Now."

"Okay, let's do it," Les said. I'll do it for Aki, he thought.

"I'll tell your mother."

Mr. Logan's smile lit up the road as they drove to the large commuter lot by the train station. Les got in the driver's seat after they parked at the end of the chain link fence that sheltered the tracks. They could hear the buzz of electricity running through the overhead wires. The second entrance behind them, the Mill Plain Road entrance, meandered up to Exit 21 of the Burr Parkway.

"Okay Les, I know you know the basics but let me do a refresher course. First thing is this. If you have your foot on the break, you're not going anywhere. Second thing is the emergency move, but it's also the beginning of every other move. It's the double stomp pull back. Both feet stomp on the clutch and the brake as you pull back the stick to center where it's free and loose. You will be in neutral and not go anywhere because of the break. The big difference between automatic and stick is really the use of both feet but you know that. Now turn on the engine," Mr. Logan said.

Les pushed in the clutch pedal and the brake. He held his feet down. The stick was released to the floating, free position, and the engine turned over.

"Good. Put it in reverse. Remember it's not in gear until the clutch is released. Do it slowly. We're flat so don't worry about the rolling. Pedal off the brake and give it a little gas. When we pull out, repeat and put it in first. Drive to the center of the lot and stop in neutral."

Les followed his father's directions, hands a little too tight on the steering wheel, but he was driving stick. He couldn't believe he was driving again and even though he fought it all the way, a smile broke through. Mr. Logan saw and couldn't fight the pride welling up.

The Fiat cut through the wind and lot. Les parked and started again but then began to drive in large loops going from first gear to second gear and back to first. The exercise was smooth and the sharp edges of anxiety never cut through into Les. They came to a stop.

"Way proud of you Les. You want to drive home?" Mr. Logan asked.

"No, there's a couple hills."

"Okay, one more time then we'll go."

Les drove around the lot a couple more times and then the roar of a strong engine overtook them. From the other side of the lot, a gray Ford Mustang was coming at them full speed heading towards the Mill Plain entrance. There were no lanes just parking spaces and Les didn't know which way to turn. The Mustang sped up.

"Right, turn right," Mr. Logan said.

Les turned right but the Mustang cut across their path and Les yanked the steering wheel left. The tall border fence that blocked the noise of the train was upon them.

"Brake," Mr. Logan said and Les's heart was shaking.

The Move, Les thought. He stomped down but his right foot slipped and hit the gas pedal. The wall grew closer. Every ounce of strength left Les's body but he lifted his foot in time and stomped the brake as hard as he could. SCREEEEECH! Thump.

Mr. Logan, not wearing his seatbelt, hit the dashboard as the car came to a hard stop.

A drip of blood came from Mr. Logan's nose as he sat back and turned to see if Les was okay. The engine idled away.

"You okay Les? Hurt?" Mr. Logan asked.

Les's fingers were bound in a tight grip on the steering wheel and had a hard time letting go as he looked over to his father. The blood on his face sparked a memory, a memory of that day when everything changed. Mr. Logan saw Les's face lose its color and the emptiness passed over his eyes.

"Are you okay?" Mr. Logan asked.

Les was frozen in place, unable to move, and the impact repeated in his thoughts. Mr. Logan reached over and shook Les's shoulder.

"Les, Les, you okay?" Mr. Logan asked.

Les looked at the steering wheel and slumped into it.

"Damn it," Mr. Logan said and pulled him back.

"Look at me. Look at me," Mr. Logan said.

Les did and just saw the blood.

"Sorry."

"What? No. Nothing to be sorry about. Anyone would have done what you did," Mr. Logan said.

"I don't want to drive anymore," Les said.

"Okay. I'll drive. You okay? Did you hurt anything?" Mr. Logan asked.

"No."

"This is my fault. I told you to turn. You did the right thing," Mr. Logan said.

"I don't want to drive anymore," Les said.

"Okay. Let's go home."

"But your nose?"

"Nose bleed, that's all, use to get them all the time. Just have to wait a couple minutes for it to stop. I'm fine."

The drive back through the even streets was silent as the street lamps flickered to life one by one. The rush of the wind was all that was heard until they pulled into the driveway. Mr. Logan cleaned up in the garage and sent Les inside. Wooly Bully spun at Les's feet but then stopped as if it sensed something was wrong. The dog looked up at him and nudged Les's hand. He petted the dog's head and somehow felt better. Wooly Bully followed him up to his room.

At his computer, Les checked his messages. There were none in any of his inboxes. He went on Facebook and posted his status: Suck at driving stick.

Eddie commented: U drove? He commented: Tried but didn't go well. She commented: At least U R trying. TTYL.

Les signed out and went on the DeviantArt and 4chan websites to check out new illustrations and forums. He then looked on io9.com and Youbentmywookie.com for reviews of independent digital comics to read. He found more than he could read in a day.

He admired much of the work and doubted that he could ever be that good. In one comic about a teenage zombie hunter named Florence, Les's eyes were drawn along the story grid without effort. The proportions of the limbs were perfect and the representation of the body in motion made the characters stand off the pages. The dialogue balloons were expertly placed to maximize both the motion of the characters and emphasize the text.

Les thought the penciler, colorist and letterer on the comic must have really communicated to get such a striking piece of graphic storytelling to come so alive. It dawned on him that all the comics and graphic novels he loved were team efforts and he no longer had a team.

A cluster of hard footsteps came from the hall and Les looked to his doorway to see his mother with a worried expression. Her lips were pressed tight.

"I have to take your father to the emergency room. He got a nose bleed and it won't stop. Let Wooly out, he hasn't gone to the bathroom in hours. I'll call you," she said and disappeared.

Les got up and went over to Wooly Bully lying on a pile of laundry. The dog lifted his front legs and Les pet his tummy.

"Thanks boy. I want to help but I can't do anything right. I'll mess everything up even worse. Maybe Eddie can do it? She can help Aki better."

Car doors closed outside and Les went to his open window and watched his mom's car drive away into the humid evening. His phone vibrated in his pocket. It was Aki.

Chapter 15: Epistles.

"Les, you have to hurry and help Rachel," Aki said.

"I tried to find her but things got messed up," Les said.

"So what. We messed up every time we drew together but we didn't stop. Please, I need your help. My minutes are running out," Aki said.

"I'll find someone else who can help you," Les said.

"There isn't anyone. My parents are in Japan and P.J. is grounded," Aki said.

"Eddie will help."

"She can't. I need you to do it. Can't explain why. You just have to go and stop Rachel from doubting herself and being afraid. Help her get on with her life, or mine really does come to an end."

"I mess everything up. I'll make it worse. Just put my dad in the hospital," Les said.

"Don't think you could mess things up anymore dipshit," Aki said.

"Dipshit?"

"Yeah, stop being one. I got to go and beware that professor."

"You told me already."

"He's like a weird next door neighbor. Crazy bro. All obsessed. Watch your back."

"Okay. Do you know if my dad will be all right?"

"I'm a ghost not psychic dude."

"Then how do you know to call when I'm about to give up?"

"Cause you're wuss, all the time. Wouldn't matter when I called."

"Dick."

"Nice one. So get off your ass and go talk to Rachel or I'll haunt you."

"Serious?"

"No, like I said I'll be going to the light side or be nothing. Seriously have to bail and keep working on Janus. Later."

The phone went dark like the power was turned off. Les closed his phone and put it in his pocket. The phone vibrated again. He took it out thinking it was Aki or his mother. It was Professor Gluck.

"Hello," Les said.

"Hello Les. Sorry for calling at this hour but I'll need you to come in early tomorrow if that's all right?"

"My Dad just went to the hospital so I don't know," Les said.

"I'm so sorry. If he is well, please come in early tomorrow. There is much to do."

"If he's okay I will," Les said.

"Excellent. If you are not able, please call me. I do hope your father will regain his health and vigor. Have a good evening," Professor Gluck said.

"Bye."

Les tossed the phone onto his bed and fell down face first onto the wrinkled sheet. Wooly Bully jumped up next to him.

"This is crazy. How am I going to pull it off?"

Wooly Bully had to go out, so Les took him to the backyard instead of walking him out front to the corner. The dog was quick to lift his leg and Wooly Bully trotted back inside. He went right over to his food bowl and looked back to Les.

"No, you mad pupster. You had dinner already."

The dog followed Les back upstairs and sat next to Les as he played World of Warcraft on his computer and waited for a call from his mother.

Midnight came and Les dozed off. Drool pooled on his shoulder and he awoke to see his fish tank screensaver active. He looked at the clock, stood up and went into the hall by Wooly Bully who was sleeping on his bed. His parents weren't home.

Les picked up his phone and saw a text from his mother.
Les,
Everything will be fine. Waiting for doctors to sign off. Home soon.
Love,
Mom

The time of the text was a half hour before so Les clicked off the lights, kicked off his Vans and went to bed. As soon as he closed his eyes, he heard the doors of his mom's car shut. Wooly Bully's ear perked up.

"It's okay Wooly. Just Mom and Dad," he said but the dog got up and barreled down the stairs to greet them.

"Now I can stretch out," Les said.

He listened to his parents creak by in the hall as they went to bed. Wooly Bully entered his room and hopped up at Les's feet. A recollection hit Les.

"Holy crap. P.J. has her email address," Les said.

Through the darkness, he shuffled over to his computer through the piles of clothes and stacks of Hulk comics on the floor. He flipped the computer on and emailed P.J. for Rachel's address. Then, he shut down the computer. The night had grace on Les as a cold front moved down from Canada and cooled the evening air. The cricket's chirps rode the sound of rustling leaves outside his window and the frogs seemed to be silenced for a moment allowing Les to finally go to sleep.

Tired eyes, corners still burdened with crust, were rubbed awake as Les awoke to the early eastern sun penetrating his window. The computer took longer than usual to boot up but Les suspected it just seemed that way because he was groggy. He signed in and there was an email from P.J. with Rachel's email address. To the bathroom he went and splashed water on his face. He had to be clear.

He walked back by a sleeping Wooly Bully, sat and typed an email with stiff fingers.

Rachel,

You don't know me but I heard about your transplant and hope you are doing well. My name is Lester Logan, I know it sounds funny, most call me L. I'm friends with Aki Kubo the person who donated his liver to you. I would like to talk with you about him and let you know what kind of person he was. I live in New Hebron and I know you live in Clover. I was just there and actually met two girls who know you. Their names were Mandy and Veronica. They said you were cool and I'd like to meet you if possible. You know, out in the open, where ever you want. I know this sounds strange but strange things are happening and I think you can help. Please let me know. Thanks.

L

Les hit the send button. All he could do was get ready to go to Professor Gluck's house. The shower was fast, even for Les, and he opened the bathroom door to see Wooly Bully sitting.

"Okay pupster, chow in a sec," Les said and the tail wagged.

Down in the kitchen the kibble rang in Wooly Bully's bowl and he gobbled it up as it hit the bottom. Not a single crumb was left. Les got some apple juice, put an ice cube in a green glass, and walked back upstairs. The ice dinged the glass like a crystal bell as Les placed it down by his keyboard. He signed into an email account and there was a reply from Rachel.

Hi Lester,

I'm sorry but we can't meet. Even though I wanted to know about my donor my parents don't want me to. I'm not allowed to go out for long anyway. I'm sorry.

Rachel

Confusion grabbed hold of Les like a hand on a leash and pulled.

"What the…?"

Les hit reply and tried to write a message but ended up deleting three versions. Wooly Bully came over and rested his chin on Les's lap. He tried to pet the dog but he jumped back and went to the door. He knew that meant Wooly Bully wanted to go outside. Les checked to see if his parents were home but they had already left for work.

"Okay Wooly. Let's go out. And hey Aki, if you have a suggestion, one would be good right about now."

Wooly Bully panted as he looked at Les from the door.

"Coming."

Les unlatched the screen door and the dog saw a few crows hopping along in the browning grass of the backyard as they pecked for worms. As soon as it was opened enough, Wooly Bully bolted out and jumped the deck stairs down to the dirt. The crows rose with caws and hard flaps of their wings. They just escaped Wooly Bully's grasp as he leapt with jaws agape. Just then, Les's phone vibrated in his pocket. It was text, a text from Aki.

Reply to Rachel with one word, Hotdog.

And so he did.

The windows and blinds of the Logan house were closed to seal in the cool of the previous night. Les thought he should chip in a few dollars to turn the AC on during the evenings of heavy heat that would soon be coming to New Hebron. He checked the clock and had a few minutes. In the kitchen, grass and doggy slobber floated in Wooly Bully's stainless steel bowl after he had lapped up most of the water, so Les poured it out in the sink and refilled the bowl. After washing his hands, Les went to his room to check for a possible reply. And there was one.

L,

How did you know about the hotdog cravings? I didn't tell anyone.
R.

Les had known Aki for years and knew the one thing he loved as much as drawing and comics was hotdogs. If any part of Aki lived on in her, it would want to eat hotdogs he figured. He replied.

R,
Let me explain in person. It would be easier. How about Pawley's in Fair Glen on Saturday at noon? It's half way between us and the hotdogs are awesome. I have to go to work now so I will respond later but I think we can help each other.
Peace,
L

The skate over to the professor's house was a blur for Les. He could only think of what Rachel would say in her reply. The professor was outside on his stoop with a cup of coffee and waved as Les rolled up. The sun beat with an unrelenting rhythm down on the quiet street and Les felt a drip of cold sweat roll down the middle of his back as he took off the roller blades on the curb.

"Hi Professor," Les said.

"Ah, I see your father is in satisfactory health if you're here," Professor Gluck said and then sipped.

"Just a nose bleed but my mom over reacts," Les said and wiped the sweat off his forehead with his free hand.

"Can't be too careful when it comes to your health. Life is too short and capricious to be otherwise. Come in there is much to do."

The basement was cool and musty. Les tugged on the front of his t-shirt to help shed the excess heat and let the cool air calm his body. He missed having air conditioning at home and sat in Cell-17 with a sigh. A piece of paper on the desk was marked with twenty spaces starting with one and ending with twenty. Next to the paper, a yellow phone that reminded Les of a raincoat sat with a pencil balanced on top of its receiver. The professor stood at the door and watched.

"Okay Les, this will sound a bit whimsical, but it is a necessary part of the study. We are going to test you for telepathic ability," Professor Gluck said and a crooked grin formed on his face.

"You believe in psychics?" Les asked.

"I don't believe in anything. I only know what the evidence presents me and there has been some strong evidence toward psychic abilities. But anything is possible and all because we don't understand a mystery now doesn't mean we won't in the future. So you know, telepathy is just one ability lumped into what many commonly call psychic abilities or ESP. Do you think psychics exist?"

"Anything is possible," Les said.

"Excellent. The phone there is a two-way, a walkie-talkie, and that's how we will conduct this test. I'm going to leave and go up stairs. We don't want you reading any body language subconsciously and when I tell you just concentrate and write down what you see in your mind. I have a list prepared and will think of the images. You just write. Okay?"

"Got it. Can I leave my phone on?" Les asked and the professor nodded.

The door was sealed and the professor went to the computer room where Lazlo scanned the internet for possible new targets. The professor pulled a yellow phone out of his pocket.

"The sensors in the helmet chamber ready?" Professor Gluck asked.

"Yes. Ready for the next test," Lazlo said.

"Good. This should prime him for the real one," Professor Gluck said.

The professor sat in a swivel chair by a window desk and gathered his papers. The list with corresponding images was placed on top of the stack in front of him.

In the cool room, Les tried to figure out how he was going to get to Pawley's if Rachel said yes and then the two-way on the desk chirped.

"First image," the professors said as his voice came through with static.

The image of a fish popped into Les's mind so he wrote it down. Another chirp came and Les saw the Eiffel Tour so he wrote it down. Twenty chirps and twenty images came and went. The test was over. At least that was what Les thought and then remembered Aki's warning. He would be on guard. For now, he waited for the professor who came a few minutes later to get the results.

Up in his swivel chair, the professor twisted back and forth and reviewed Les's answers. He checked twice. He checked a third time. His yellow pencil slammed to the desk and rolled into a patch of sunlight.

"He got thirteen out of twenty Lazlo."

"That's crazy. I don't know anyone who got more than two."

"He got thirteen."

"What do we do?"

"We proceed as planned. His elevated abilities might be why the spectral unit attached to him. Just get the sensors ready and the EM trap set. I'll deal with it."

Les could hear the footsteps echo outside of the room and then they stopped. The professor opened the door with smile like a crescent moon. An itch grew on Les's knees and he couldn't help but scratch. The professor noticed.

"You all right? Allergies?" Professor Gluck asked.

"No, just itchy. How'd I do?"

"Sorry to say my boy but you did straight average. Nothing to be ashamed of. The next phase will be taking place in the cell, I mean chamber, where you used the Koren helmet."

"Do I get to wear it again? It was kind of cool."

"No, you just need to relax in the comfy chair there," Professor Gluck said and waved for Les to follow.

The pencil fell off the desk as Les got up. As he placed it back on the table, Les checked his pocket to make sure his phone was still there. Into the chamber Les went and almost snickered because he couldn't believe he was getting paid to hang out in the AC and chill in a Lazy-boy. Professor Gluck followed close behind.

The recliner creaked when Les plopped in and grabbed hold of the armrests. On the corner table were three plain envelopes marked A, B, and C. On the rickety table next to the recliner was a pad and pen.

"Okay Les, what I want you to do is wait for me to leave and then get up and grab those envelopes. What you do next, and this sounds strange, is sit back in the seat and invoke a deceased relative or friend. Ask them to tell you what word is written in the envelope by sending a signal or image to your brain," Professor Gluck said.

Les's face puckered.

"What? I'm not doing that. That's not cool," Les said.

"It is necessary. I assure you."

"Why?"

"If I tell you then the data could be corrupted."

"Then I'm not doing this. You can pay half of what you owe me and I'll be on my way," Les said.

"Fine, I guess the results are all that matter. We are testing the perception of singularity in opposition to multiplicity through a perceived collective state versus an isolated state. Simply, does the belief that one is connected to others in an unending existence allow humans to tap into a collective consciousness in the quantum state and acquire non-linear information? Or, does it do nothing? That's the test."

"Oh, okay," Les said and thought it sounded scientific enough.

"Good. Pad and paper are on the table and please invoke the same entity each time. We found vocalization is best instead of just thinking it. Allow a minute to pass between each invocation. You are being recorded. Red light up there in the corner."

"Fine. Was that there last time?" Les asked.

"No, just installed it for this set of experiments. I'll be back in ten minutes."

Upstairs Lazlo gave full power to the Forward Looking Infrared (FLIR) camera so that heat signatures could be detected. The induction amplifier hidden under the recliner that boosted electromagnetic field was turned on and so was the electronic voice phenomenon recorder. The electromagnetic field detector was ready and had been for an hour.

The professor walked over to Lazlo and stood behind him to watch the monitor.

"Hope that FLIR camera catches an anomaly. If the theory holds that spirits absorb energy to manifest, therefore making everything around them cold, this would help prove your theory about consciousness and energy similitude," Lazlo said.

"We can only hope. Here he goes. He's picking up the first envelope."

The envelope gave Les some trouble and fell down to the floor. He picked it up and fell back into the seat. He closed his eyes and shook his head.

"Can't believe I'm doing this. Aki what's in this envelope? Send me an image."

The cool was nice, too nice, Les thought and waited. No images came at first but then he saw a bear trap close in his mind. In his right pocket, the phone vibrated.

"Crap."

The phone slipped out of his pocket with ease. Les sheltered it from the view of the camera but he didn't know the FLIR camera hidden in the metal wall cabinets behind him was focused on his right side.

Upstairs, the professor watched Les reach for his phone on the infrared video feed showing Les's face as a red hot spot and the rest of his body as yellows, blues and purples. A large cold patch of deep blue was hovering next to Les and the professor slapped Lazlo's arm.

"Look," he said to Lazlo.

Les flipped open the phone and saw that he got a text from Aki.

B-ware. Lie about pics.

The message was deleted. Les faked a cough and hunched over so he could put the phone back in his pocket. He wrote down Ferris Wheel for A. The ruse was repeated and Les wrote down Aardvark for B. The final time he wrote Taj Mahal for C and gave a thumbs up to show he was done. He felt like a dork once again.

Behind the door, the professor forced a smile. He opened it and bound inside.

"Let's see how you did?" he said and picked up the envelopes.

The professor took out a pen knife. It shimmered under the light as it sliced the seal.

"Okay, A was a hunter with an orange vest and you wrote…?" Professor Gluck asked.

Les picked up the pad and flipped it open and next to A was Ferris Wheel.

"Didn't get that one," Les said and noticed the professor's eyebrows lower and his smile went flat.

They went over the other two results. The professor frowned and shook his head in disappointment. The professor knew that the cold spot in the FLIR video was indeed Akihide Kubo but why did Les get the answers wrong? Professor Gluck dismissed Les and went up to talk to Lazlo who was behind the computer monitor watching the video again and going over the sensor data.

"Professor, something was in the room. The EM field detector spiked. And the FLIR picked it up but no EVP. No voices but Les's," Lazlo said and spun to look at the professor who at that moment had a revelation.

"Can you hack Les's deleted message in his phone like you said?"

"Sure but not for long. They remain as smoke in the system for just a bit," Lazlo said.

"Do it. Quick. Hurry."

Lazlo found the message. They both read it.

"It seems he was there. Set the trap. When Les comes here next, we'll capture the proof we need."

Chapter 16: Buses and hotdogs.

The day turned for the hotter. Bare feet would blister on contact with asphalt. The road was soft and gave under the wheels of Les's roller blades as he streaked through the wall of light that fell like molten sun. Most of the even streets were shaded to either side by old growth maples but a few new lanes he traveled were exposed to the sunlight. Nothing concerned Les other than Rachel's reply however, not the heat, not the building traffic.

Wooly Bully heard the familiar grind of roller blades coming from around the corner outside and began running through the house in a frantic search. Toenails tapped and scratched the hardwood floors as the dog looked through every open window he could reach until he stopped at the window by the front door. The dog's tail began to wag in quick circles. As Les came through the door, roller blades in hand, Wooly Bully reared up and put his paws on Les's shoulders.

"Damn boy, you're almost as tall as me. Down," Les said and Wooly Bully gave his chin a lick just for good measure before hitting the floor.

The dog followed Les upstairs. His toenails clacked and scraped the shine off the hardwood floors. The computer couldn't boot up quick enough for Les as he scratched his knees. The web browser came up and in a few clicks so did his email. His eyes widened as he nodded his head.

"Well, one good thing Wooly. Going to Pawley's, but the bad thing is how to get there?"

He called Eddie and she was busy with a job interview with a photographer that day. Les didn't want his parents to know what he was doing so the one other option presented itself. He had to ride the bus on a Saturday, something Les never wanted to do.

...

Les didn't think the bus stop was all that bad on the clear Saturday morning. It was nice out and no one was there. When he looked up the public transportation website for the county the night before, he found the fare was only two dollars and fifty cents to get him Fair Glen right down the street from Pawley's.

He stood on the Old Post Road and waited for the bus that coughed diesel exhaust to pull up to the curb. The door retracted with a whoosh and a thud. Les got in and four stops came and went on the empty bus, empty all save one kid in the back wearing all black. Les could hear the music blare from his earphones seven rows up. Soon, the stop for Beechnut Avenue came into view. Les knew Beechnut Avenue well from driving it to hockey practice on all those early mornings with his father.

The bus stopped and the doors opened with a gush of hot air radiating off the road. Les stepped out and before him was the gradual rise of the Goldfield Hill where the beacon of hotdog goodness named Pawley's crowned the top. A refurbished red barn with a screened in patio had a line out the door marked Take Out.

The world was perfumed with hints of pungent sauerkraut and fried onions but nothing, not even the car exhaust on Beechnut Avenue, could compete with the scent of hotdogs topped on the griddle with a blend of butter and secret ingredients. In the past, many a foodie was brought to tears before Les's eyes when they bit into their first Pawley's dog. Les and Aki knew the key was the bun that was buttered on the inside and toasted. Les wished Aki could have another foot long with him as he made his way to the packed parking lot.

His cell phone said noon but Les didn't see anyone resembling Rachel outside or on the patio. She must be inside in the autographed section he thought. Drooling customers who were leaving with white paper bags warm with hot dogs and twice fried fries blocked Les's path. He made it up a set of side stairs and to the back of the restaurant. There a row of intimate booths stained dark with time, that the locals called the Autograph Pews, lined a plank wall covered in names carved right in the wood by patrons. Some of the carvings were old, some were just scratches, some were deep, some even had dates going back to the Seventies.

To his left was a service window where the clerk gave the sit down customers their orders and conducted the orchestra of cooking played out for all to see and hear. The fire, smoke and sizzle was a melody riding the rhythm of spatulas and forks clanging on the metal surfaces of the counters and griddle. Les took a big whiff and then made his way up the row of booths.

At the last booth beside the coat rack, Rachel sat. Her curly hair was pulled back revealing a slender neck. Les thought her tan was too dark for so early in the summer.

He couldn't fight it. Les had to scratch his knee while he walked over to her. Be like P.J., he thought and stood up straight with his head held high.

"Rachel?"

"Les," she said and looked up to him.

"Can I?" Les asked and pointed to the empty seat

"Yeah."

The bench was hard and pock marked from years of people digging their knives into it. It made for a bumpy seat. Les forgot to breathe for a second as Rachel looked at him with amber eyes tempered with depth and experience. She rubbed circles on the top of her other hand that was flat on the table. Les took a breath and coughed.

"Sorry, this is awkward," he said.

"It's more than awkward," she said.

"Did you order?" Les asked and pulled over a laminated menu in a wire stand next to the condiments.

"Not sure if I'm going to stay. Will you answer a question?" she asked.

"Sure."

"How'd you know about hot dogs?" she asked.

Les froze. He hadn't thought about that but then he recalled a story he read about a man in Pittsburgh who had a heart transplant. The man craved avocado.

"I read that some people who get transplants crave foods or want to do things that their donors liked. Aki loved hot dogs more than anything besides drawing," he said.

"He was an artist?"

"A good one. The reason I contacted you was to let you know that Aki was my best friend and now his cells live in you and I'll do anything to help him and you."

"That's sweet of you but I don't need any help. I'm not really doing anything right now," she said and looked down to the table.

"Then that's what I'll help you with. You need to do something," he said.

"That's kind but I don't know you," she said.

"Let's hang out and change that. Anywhere. Up to you. Please just tell me what you want to do to be happy."

"How do you know I'm not happy?" she asked.

"I uh figured…"

"You figured what?"

"I don't know. Just let me help you live and not be guilty about Aki."

"How'd you know I felt guilty?" she asked and leaned in.

"Uh, I just figured…"

"There you go again, just figuring," she said.

Rachel clasped her hands on the table. Les held his breath and started to gouge his knees. He closed his eyes for a second and stopped scratching. Les leaned in and looked at her with all the sincerity he could muster.

"I'm sorry if I upset you but…"

"That's okay. I'm just overwhelmed. You come out of nowhere with all of this and I haven't been out in months so I'm a little nervous," she said.

"Why are you nervous?"

"My parents are over my shoulder all the time. They really cramp me. I told them I was just driving to library. Why the hell am I telling you this?"

"Because a part of you is my friend."

"What was he like?" she asked.

"He saved me from myself. He could draw a free hand circle perfect every time. He learned to play the cello so his parents would let him play guitar. We were going to become famous comic book creators. You know be both artists and writers. Aki also had an Ebay business where he bought and sold collectibles from art glass to action figures," Les said.

"Wow. I'm a musician too, a singer, or was actually. Sounds like he did a lot," she said.

"He was driven. That's for sure. Now he's helping you live and I want to help too. Just wondering, did you graduate?" he asked.

"Yes. Finished up before regular school actually, but my mom didn't want me going to graduation because they were afraid I'd get an infection. I'm on drugs that suppress my immune system so I don't reject the liver," she said and looked back down at the table.

"Going to college?" he asked.

"I got into NYU but my parents don't think I can handle the strain and we declined. I don't know if I can handle school or not," she said.

"How about going to Upton for a few classes to start out and then transfer?"

"My parents are afraid I will get sick."

"Do you think you'll get sick?"

"I don't know. I don't think so but maybe."

"Do you want to go?"

"Yes."

"Then maybe that's why I'm here to help. To get you to college," Les said.

At that moment hard footsteps pounded down the aisle

"Rachel! What are you doing here?" a huge man with a bushy moustache asked.

Les assumed it was her father and braced himself.

"Dad. How did…?"

"The GPS unit in you car has a tracking unit. I never thought I'd have to use it but I drove by the library and your car wasn't there. Who's this?" Mr. Higgs asked.

"I'm Les sir."

"Well Les you better get going," Mr. Higgs said.

"Dad, he was a friend of my donor. His name was Aki," she said.

Mr. Higgs face dropped. He stepped back and slowly lifted his hand.

"That information was closed. No one was to know that. How'd you find that out? How'd you find my daughter? What the hell are you doing?" he asked with a finger pointed right at Les.

Les crouched into the corner by the window as Mr. Higgs stood at the end of the table and his finger was on Les like a gun sight.

"I'm just trying to help your daughter sir," Les said.

"Well you're not. Get out of here before I call the cops and have a restraining order placed," he said.

"I just want to help you Rachel," Les said and Mr Higgs yanked him out of the seat.

"Leave," Mr Higgs said.

"Fine," Les said

"Rachel we're going home. You could get sick," Mr. Higgs said.

Les looked back over his shoulder and saw her watching him.

...

The bus ride back was long. Les was filled with the sense of failure. He couldn't help anyone.

At home, Les walked through the front door and Wooly Bully sensed his sadness and just walked up to him and sat.

"Hey buddy," he said and knelt down.

Les pet the dog with long strokes and held back the tears bulging in his eyes. He heard his mother in the kitchen and didn't want her to see him like that so he bolted upstairs with Wooly Bully right behind.

The cell phone was tossed on his bed and Les turned on his computer. With dread he turned to look at the phone thinking Aki was going to call any second. He checked his emails. One was from Eddie and another was from Rachel. He opened that one first.

L,

Sorry about my dad. He's just scared. But he brought up something at Pawley's that bothered me on the drive home and if we're going to be friends you have to be honest with me. What's the real story of how you know so much? And also thanks for trying to help. So?

R

Les was tired of making things up but telling her everything could end their contact. He swiveled in his chair and looked at Wooly Bully burying his face in his pile of socks.

"Aki, give me sign," Les said.

No sign came.

Mrs. Logan was outside in the hall listening. She turned around and quietly walked away hoping her son would be his old self one day.

Les scratched his knees. He rubbed his chin. His mind was blank. There was only way to convince Rachel to get on with her life. He had to tell her the truth and let her know Aki gave her his blessing. Les decided to omit the part about how Aki only had a limited time. Almost the whole story, six paragraphs worth, was written and sent. The fragile outcome depended on her believing an incredible tale that Les himself wouldn't believe if it didn't happen to him.

The wait for the reply was slow. Every second seemed like the last drop of water that wouldn't drip from the faucet, hanging on for dear life, and Les could only think of one thing that sped time along. He pulled out his old sketch pad and drew eyes, hands, and hair in pencil.

Three pages were filled and Les spun around to Wooly Bully and held out the pad for the dog to see.

"Look Pupster, my hands are getting better."

The dog looked up but then away and scratched his snout with the side of his paw and licked it.

"I see."

Les opened his email and there was a reply. His stomach churned and shrunk. He couldn't force a deep breath so he just balled up his hands in fists.

"Just do it man."

He opened the email.

L,

That would explain it and I don't think you're insane. I had dreams about a Japanese guy for a while and it's true that nobody knew who my donor was besides my doctor. I called. I want to help but I don't know what to do. I'm stuck here and can't do anything.

R

Les knew exactly what to write.

R,

That's what he wants to change.

L

He hit send and a moment later a reply came.

L,

Don't get me wrong, I want to do things but I don't know if I can. My dad took away my car too.

R

Les was stuck. He didn't know what to do either but the unread email from Eddie caught his attention and he thought what would she do? The day of Aki's memorial when Eddie picked him up to go out popped into his head. It was the night when he thought of his grandmother May who went to the Buddy Holly concert and sparks of inspiration crackled through his brain.

Les replied.

We'll take trip into the city & C a band. If U can survive the crowds, the noise & the city then U can survive anything. College would B nothing after that. Friend me on Facebook please so we can chat easier. I'd say text but that costs & IM on this sucks. The concert will be fun.

       L

He then remembered that Rachel mentioned she was a singer and read that she was in band. A plan came to him that seemed almost perfect but he knew perfect wasn't possible.

Chapter 17: One.

The phone rang on his bed. Les just knew it had to be Aki. He couldn't wait to tell him the news that he'd be going to the bright side soon. It was Eddie.

"Hey Eddie, what's up?"

"Lots L," she said.

"What's with the photographer? Get the gig?" he asked.

"So I guess you didn't read my email then? Explains it," she said.

"What's wrong? You sound sad."

"Sort of, well I got the job but I have to ditch town for the summer," she said.

"What? Why?"

"The photographer, Cabal, is doing a photo-journalism tour of car shows across the US. I get paid. I travel. And, I'm away from mom," she said.

"But I need your help."

"No, you don't."

"Aki needs your help. You can't go."

"Aki doesn't need me. He contacted you and I have to go."

"When?"

"Tomorrow."

"What the hell am I going to do?"

"What you have been. Sorry I can't be around, but things happen for a reason and they take me on another path. Not like I'm leaving forever. Just two months."

"That's the whole summer."

"It's lame that I don't have time to lounge, but hey, you don't have time either. Got to bounce and you'll do great. I know. I had a dream you would. Bye," Eddie said.

"Bye," Les said and pressed the button.

He made it to his chair and spun as he looked at the ceiling. His heart beat felt stiff.

"This is going to be harder without her help Wooly."

The phone rang again. The world continued to spin as he got up from the chair and hobbled over to the bed. He just answered.

"Hello."

"Les, it's Professor Gluck."

"Hi professor. What's wrong?"

"Nothing, I was wondering if you could come over for an added session?"

"For added money sure."

"An extra forty be okay?"

"Sure. What time?"

"Ten would be perfect."

"Ten is good. I'll be there."

"See you then."

"Bye."

Les turned to Wooly Bully, his eyes half closed, and shrugged. The dog closed his eyes.

A balmy morning brewed and Les told his parents that he was going to work at Professor Gluck's house. Wooly Bully paced and tried to get Les's attention as he got ready. The dog ran in front of Les when he went to the front door and blocked his way.

"Not now Wooly. I have to jet. Move," Les said and stepped by the dog.

He bolted out the door in a shot and was down the even streets gliding along through Sunday morning drivers. He hoped there would still be tickets for the Snaggle Toothed Gauchos who were playing at the Palladian in a few days. They were the only band he wanted to see that he could find online the night before. Les figured they were a good band and that most girls liked them. He needed to find a way to get Rachel to the train since her parents would probably track her car. At least she friended him on Facebook though and told him she wanted to go to the concert. He thought that was a good start.

Les pulled out his phone when he passed the college and checked the time as he skated along. Sweat formed on his brow and began to drip down. He was late and skated with his head down as fast as he could. A box truck bounced and rumbled along so Les cut across the street and grabbed the bumper. A free ride for a mile and enough momentum to carry him almost all the way to Brookside Lane was a relief for his tired legs.

As Les turned the corner, he could see the professor standing on his front stoop with his arms crossed. He didn't think he looked too happy.

"A bit on the tardy side aren't we?" Professor Gluck said as Les rolled to a stop.

"Sunday drivers in the way. You know," Les said.

"Come in. There is much to discuss."

Les followed the professor through the house, the shades all drawn, and down to the basement. At the bottom of the stairs, the professor turned and looked at Les.

"You have your phone?" he asked.

"Yes. Why? You want me to turn it off?" Les asked.

"Oh no, it has an important role to play today. Very important," he said and waved Les on.

The door to Cell-17 was open and Les was ushered inside. Lazlo shuffled over from down the hall eating an apple. The juice dripped out of the corners of his mouth. He wiped his chin with the back of his hand. The professor stood in the doorway and Les could hear a buzz outside. Lazlo stood behind the professor and took out a hand held device from his pocket. He tapped the screen and the buzz went off with a hard thump. The professor pulled out a digital video recorder from his lab coat pocket.

"You mind if we film this session?" he asked.

"Sure. Go ahead. You're paying," Les said.

"Excellent. My dear boy you don't know just how important you are. You are going to be a part of the greatest scientific discovery in history," he said.

"How kids' brains develop? The perception thing?" Les asked.

"Not exactly. I need you to call your friend Akihide," he said.

"What?"

"Yes, you heard me, call your friend Akihide," he said.

"He's dead."

"Yes I know, but he is in contact with you. We have proof. That last experiment where we had you invoke a spirit for psychic guidance was a test to see if he would come if you called for him. He did," he said.

"What? No he didn't. He didn't call me," Les said and moved to the door.

The professor held his hand up.

"So he does call you. Sit down. Now," he said.

"No. I'm out," Les said.

"No you're not. My funding is going to be cut soon and I need evidence. If you want your money, you'll sit. This is a great opportunity to make history Les. You'll be famous and I'll help you with anything you need regarding your friend Akihide. Anything," he said.

"I don't know what evidence I can give you," Les said.

"Just get him to call you and we'll do the rest," he said.

"Guess it can't hurt and I can use the help," Les said.

He sat down, pulled out his phone and spun it on the table.

"Here goes. Aki dude, need you to call me. Professor said he'd help us. You need to call me please," Les said.

The professor's eyes focused on Les and they waited. Nothing happened for three minutes of silence.

"Try again and this time tell him you won't help unless he calls you," Professor Gluck said.

"That won't work," Les said.

"Try. Now," he said.

"No, I won't say that but I'll give it another shot. Aki, bro, call me. This guy said he'd help us," Les said.

The professor rubbed his hands in front of him and Lazlo stood behind with the device in his hand. The phone then vibrated and moved along the table. Les picked up the phone and looked to see who it was. Lazlo tapped the touch screen to the hand held device and the buzz returned.

"Sorry, it's my mom" Les said and answered the phone but no one answered.

"Weird, dropped the call," Les said.

The professor looked over his shoulder and Lazlo tapped the device again and the buzzing stopped.

"Maybe you should call her back?" Professor Gluck asked.

"Probably or she won't stop calling," Les said.

"Before you do, you need to know all this is confidential. You can't tell anyone," Professor Gluck said.

"Okay."

Les called.

"Phone working?" Professor Gluck asked.

"Fine."

The professor looked back at Lazlo and winked as Les connected with his mother.

"What's up Mom?" Les asked and looked to the floor.

"Where?" Les said and his hands began to shake.

"Where? Where?" Les asked.

Les's face went blank and he turned to the professor.

"I'll be right there," Les said.

"Everything all right?" Professor Gluck asked.

"No. I have to go," Les said.

"But we need to continue," Professor Gluck said.

"I'll be back if you promise to help Aki, but I have to go. I have to go now," Les said.

"Okay, I promise. Go. We'll complete this as soon as you can," Professor Gluck said.

Les couldn't remember putting his roller blades on or skating two miles with his Adidas in hand toward his house. He sped to the King's Highway Veterinary Hospital, a plain brick building at a four way stop. Inside his mother, her white blouse stained with blood, stood at the front desk signing forms. A man with a green cat carrier sat on the wooden bench that lined the waiting room. The cat meowed non stop. Les didn't take off the roller blades and rolled over to his mother. She spun around and saw his face. Her lips quivered.

"He got out. I don't know how but he got out," she said.

"What happened?" Les asked.

"Got a call from the person who hit him with their car. We rushed over. Picked him up and took him here. Your father went in with Wooly and the vet. Been twenty minutes," she said.

A set of double doors swung open. Mr. Logan came out with Wooly Bully's collar. His head was down, staring at the collar, as he shuffled out in a daze to the waiting room. He looked up to his wife with a face bereft of joy and color.

"He's gone. He's gone," Mr. Logan said and dropped the collar.

Mrs. Logan covered her mouth with both hands but a gasp slipped through to betray her pain. Les rolled back a foot and looked at the polished floor where a tangle of gray fur spun up into his wheel.

"Wooly followed me to work. He followed me. He died because of me. People die when they follow me," Les said and his eyes went empty as he looked up to the exit sign.

Mr. Logan picked up the collar and walked over. He grabbed Les's shoulders.

"No. He didn't die because of you. You didn't do anything. Not your fault," Mr. Logan said and choked back his tears for second but couldn't hold back.

The family grieved and the meows of the frightened cat ricocheted off the tile floor. A cloud covered the sun and the world outside dimmed.

Chapter 18: Dirty laundry.

Professor Gluck and Lazlo went to organize and review the old data upstairs. Lazlo fired up the computer. The professor grabbed his chair and pulled up next to him. Each was confident. Each was relaxed. The thick clouds covering the sun outside didn't darken their mood.

"Pull up the EVP's first. I want to hear that voice again," Professor Gluck said.

"Gottcha," Lazlo said, cracked his knuckles and his fingertips flew over the keyboard.

He leaned in closer to the monitor. His eyes narrowed.

"What? That can't be right," Lazlo said.

"What?" Professor Gluck asked.

"The files are gone," Lazlo said.

"Are you sure?"

"They were saved in a specific folder to keep them safe from prying eyes and the folder is gone," Lazlo said and looked over his shoulder at the professor's worried face.

"Check again."

"I checked three times and three anonymous junk folders too. They're gone," Lazlo said.

"Check the FLIR recordings. If those infrared heat image recordings of the entity hovering by Les are gone too, we're done for."

"We can start over," Lazlo said and looked at the professor with a confused expression.

"No. Got an email from Dean Maecenus yesterday. We get this together or I'm going to be teaching intro psych at a community college. Don't look at me, find the recordings."

"On it," Lazlo said.

The professor rubbed circles with his fingertips on his temples and Lazlo searched. Though it was cool in the room, both men began to sweat. A bead of perspiration trickled down Lazlo's forehead to the tip of his nose and dripped down onto the keyboard. He never noticed and the search ended.

"It's all gone. All the files related to Les. Every single one. On the hard drive and on the backup external hard drive, it's all been deleted," Lazlo said.

The professor went limp in his chair. He tilted back his head and looked at the ceiling.

"Damn it. We looked at the FLIR files earlier before Les got here. That means one of two things happened. Either the consciousness of Akihide Kubo is interfering or the computer was hacked," Professor Gluck said.

"How could the computer be hacked? This one isn't connected to the internet," Lazlo said.

"That leaves us on option. We have to do whatever it takes to trap the consciousness of Akihide Kubo in the EM field. If we don't, years of research and work are gone."

...

The night came on deep clouds rolling in from the west.

At dinner in the Logan household, there were more tears wiped from sad faces than conversation. Les kept expecting the cold wet nose to nudge his leg until he snuck Wooly Bully a piece of bread. Mrs. Logan cleared the table in the breakfast nook and looked at Mr. Logan as she went to the kitchen. He nodded. Les stared at the condensation coat his cool glass of water. He drew an arrow on the glass with his finger.

"Les, I don't want to upset you anymore than you are. We're all upset but you said something we need to address," Mr. Logan said.

"What? I didn't say anything?"

"Not at dinner, at the vet's," Mr. Logan said.

"What?"

"You said people follow you and die. What do you mean?" Mr. Logan asked and turned his chair to face Les.

"I don't remember saying that."

"You did. Your mother and I both heard you. What does it mean?" he asked.

"I don't remember saying it. I don't know."

"Please Les, we need to talk about this," Mr. Logan said.

He reached for Les's hand but Les pulled away.

"I don't know what I said. I'm going to my room," Les said.

"Okay, okay, this has been a rough day for all of us. We'll talk when you are able. I love you Les," Mr. Logan said.

"Going to my room."

Wooly Bully's scent clung to Les's piles of clothes. He looked at his bed and saw a few stray dog hairs on the scrunched up blue sheet. Les couldn't feel anything but the world around him shrunk.

"Can't live like this," Les said.

Les could see himself pick up the piles of clothes and carry them down to the laundry room but he wasn't controlling his actions. He heard his parents talk but it sounded like they had plastic cups covering their mouths. Up and down he went with five loads of wash. His mother watched him and knew it was bad sign. He cleaned his room after Aki died.

Les took his box of first issue comics, boarded and never taken out of the plastic sleeves, and slipped it into his closet jammed with winter jackets and then collected all of the comics he had spread out across his room. On his bed he put Marvel titles with Marvel titles, DC with DC, Dark Horse with Dark Horse and independent with independent. A Thor comic topped off the Marvel stack with cover crawling with lightning bolts. A Batman comic with the Joker's face on the cover slid off the top of the DC stack. The Dark Horse pile dominated by Hellboy comics tilted and then spilled on to the floor.

"Great. Can't seem to keep anything together," Les said and then bent over to pick up the glossy comics. Under his bed, two rogue comics caught his eyes. Les slide them out with his fingertips and snickered.

"That's were Chew went," he said and was reminded of the day he and Aki went to Dark Light Comics in downtown New Hebron before it closed. While still bent over, he flipped through the pages Chew: Issue Three, and smiled.

"Hey Aki, remember this. It's the only comic we never argued over. You liked the psychic who got visions by eating something and I liked the art. Seemed like so long ago. All right. Back to work," he said and got back to cleaning.

Standing on a clear floor, Les swept up the dirt around the New York Rangers rug his father bought when he picked up his first hockey stick at five years old. He hadn't seen it in months with all of the laundry piled on it. Les poured the grime from the dustpan into his tin trash can. With an armful of used paper for the recycle bin and his trash can, Les went to the garage and put the rubbish with the rest in the corner.

When he got back upstairs, he heard his phone vibrate and saw it skip across his desk. Les stopped it from falling off the edge of the desk but just held his hand there and stared at the phone. He thought why can't I pick it up? Feel like I'm on auto-pilot.

Les closed his eyes, took a deep breath and bit his lip. He rolled his neck and opened his eyes. The phone continued to vibrate and he picked it up. It was Aki but for the first time Les wasn't nervous about talking to a ghost.

"Yo dude," Les said.

"Snap out of it bro. I need you to focus," Aki said.

"I can't help you man. People die if they follow me. I'll just tell Rachel the whole truth. She'll be fine. I'm sorry. I'm so sorry," Les said.

"Dude if you ditch her, she not going to be fine," Aki said.

"Sure she will. But if she follows me she'll get messed up."

"No she won't. This is why I called. I told you it's okay between us remember?" Aki asked.

"Yeah."

"Do you believe me?" Aki asked.

"Yeah."

"Good. Dude, what happened to me wasn't your fault. I didn't blindly follow your orders. I made the decision to go to the reservoir. There was nothing you did or could have done that would have changed anything," Aki said.

"I saw you bleeding. I saw your head all crushed. I tried to pull you out but couldn't."

"I know bro," Aki said.

"I'm sorry Aki."

"Don't be. I'm sorry you had to go through that," Aki said.

"I'm going to mess it up Aki."

"No you won't. Listen, you have to take Rachel to that concert. Great idea by the way," Aki said.

"I'm scared. I don't want to hurt anyone," Les said.

"You're not going to. You're going to save me bro."

Right then, Les blinked a slow blink. A connection was made in his thoughts and the world got a bit lighter.

"Save you. Yeah, I've got to save you and I know how," Les said

"I don't have much time."

"I have a plan, and if it doesn't work, I have another," Les said.

"I suspected you would. You are the better storyteller. So, want to share?" Aki asked.

"And destroy the suspense, hell no," Les said.

"Cool. Well, I have to go and remember we only have three minutes of cell time left."

"Dude, is Wooly Bully with you?" Les asked.

"I don't know. Dogs seem to be in between worlds anyway and living dogs react to spirits just like the spirit of a dog would. I'll keep an eye for him. And dude, beware the professor. He's not right in the head."

"I will," Les said.

Chapter 19: Elemental

The next morning arrived like the end of a song and Les was not going to let what happened stops efforts. The weather forecast was checked online. Even though dark clouds filled the sky outside Les's window, there was only a forty percent chance of rain or thunderstorm. He called the professor and asked to resume the experiment. Les figured if the study revealed the truth then it would help everyone and the professor wasn't really dangerous, just odd. Plus, he needed the money for the concert tickets. He was across town as fast as his roller blades could carry him.

The professor wasn't waiting outside on his stoop. Instead, Lazlo got out of his Prius that was parked by the curb as Les rolled up the slate walkway. He waved. The pewter light sifted down from the overcast above and made Lazlo look like a zombie to Les.

"Hey kid," Lazlo said and put a hoop of keys in his pocket.

"Hi. What's up?" Les asked.

"History in the making kid. History," Lazlo said.

"Okay," Les said, sat on the stone stair and pulled off his roller blades. He placed them out of view besides the stairs behind a juniper bush.

"And you just fell into it. Lucky kid," Lazlo said and stepped by.

The front door opened and Professor Gluck let Lazlo enter without a word.

"So glad you came back today. Shall we get started?"

"Sure professor. Uh, one question," Les said.

"Okay."

"Can I have my money now? I need it. Since you lied to me and all I thought…"

"That's all? Sure you can have the money. I'll get it. Meet me downstairs."

"Cool," Les said.

The cool air refreshed Les as he went downstairs and sat in Cell-17. The desk was bare. No pencil. No papers. The sound of Les scratching his dry knees was the only noise besides his breath. In moments, the professor appeared in the door and tossed Les an envelope thick with cash.

"It's all there. I'm going to record the session. Is that all right?" Professor Gluck asked.

"Sure," Les said.

Lazlo appeared behind the professor and once more had the device in his hand. The small video camera was pulled out of the professor's lab coat and he lifted it to his right eye as he approached Les.

"Entry Les Logan. The time code is set and in sync with the other recording equipment. Just want you to respond to a set of questions. All right?" Professor Gluck asked.

"Sure," Les said.

Lazlo stepped into the doorway and watched Les with hawk eyes.

"Question one. Do you believe in ghosts?"

"Yes."

"Two. Have you ever seen a ghost?"

"Technically no."

"Three. Have you ever communicated with a ghost?"

"Yes."

The camera lens focused on Les's face and Lazlo step through the doorway.

"Four. How did you communicate with the ghost?"

"I talked to him on my cell phone."

Lazlo closed the door and the professor bumped into the table as he got closer.

"Five. Can you contact the ghost?"

"I did once. Yes."

"Good. Did you know the ghost when he was living?"

"Yes professor," Les said.

"Does the ghost want you to do something and are you going to do it?"

"Yes but it's only to help someone else," Les said.

His forehead wrinkled with suspicion. Les didn't like how the questions were going.

"Would you say you hear his voice?"

"Uh yes, I said I talked to him through my phone," Les said and put his hands flat on the table.

The chair rattled as Les scooted it back and crossed his arms. Lazlo went over to the wall behind the professor and put his ear to it. It seemed odd to Les. Spikes of heat ran down his back. His hands started to shake with an adrenaline surge. Something was wrong just as Aki had warned him. Les summoned courage or fear, he didn't know which, and uncrossed his arms and stood up.

"I don't like this. It feels weird and way too cramped with three of us in here. Before I answer anything else, you need to tell me what's up?" Les said.

"You know almost everything but let me tell you something you didn't know. My theory is that human consciousness, or as primitive people call it a soul, consists of quantum entangled strings of energy that inhabit a series of electrical matrices. Simply put, everything in this universe is made of energy. Matter is just a compact and evolved form of energy hence E equals MC squared. But this energy is made of tiny vibrating strings. When stretched they look like strings but when observed they look like a particle. These strings all are connected at the tiniest of levels, smaller than atoms, and when some of the strings communicate together across distances it's called quantum entanglement or what Einstein called 'spooky action at a distance'," Professor Gluck said.

Les put his hands on the table and tilted his head to look up at the professor.

"Across distance?" Les asked.

"So what happens to one part of the string happens to all of the strings instantaneously. So I think these entangled networks of energy are able to inhabit a series of electrical pathways like a spider web that is stretched out and connected to individual points. This way it's able to maintain itself with external energy. That's what I must prove," Professor Gluck said.

"So the human soul is a spider web of energy bound to the brain since it electrical too?" Les asked.

"Exactly, but outside of the corporeal realm there is a massive field of consciousness where each soul, or spectral unit, is created and eventually returns."

Lazlo then walked over to the other wall and put his ear up to it. Les sat back down and scratched his eyebrow. The camera panned out to get Les fully in frame.

"What about psychics hearing the dead and telepathy between twins?" Les asked. Lazlo pulled his ear away and turned to look at the professor with wide eyes.

"That is due to the quantum entanglement. All things are connected on the quantum level and everything that can happen eventually will. But to answer your query, I think that twins' consciousnesses might not be totally disconnected from each other, so what one thinks, the other might be able to pick up. Quantum entanglement can act across any distance. And as for psychics, it is possible for a non-corporeal being, a spectral unit, sorry, a soul to connect a part of its consciousness to a person who has a unique brain that allows for a bonding. But, I really don't know," Professor Gluck said.

Lazlo lifted up the hand held device and tapped the professor on the shoulder.

"That's my signal Les. We can begin now."

"Why can Aki call me?" Les asked.

"Now that cell phones have more advanced circuits, memory and more powerful batteries they mimic human brains enough to allow the separated consciousness to utilize them. Anything with an electrical grid can be used by these spectral units I theorize, and that's why people have reported phenomenon with TV's, lights going on and off, communicating with the dead over the internet and so on."

Lazlo tapped the professor's shoulder harder.

"Fine Lazlo. What I need you to do Les is to call Aki. We have cameras set up to detect his presence. Have him manifest for us. If we do it a few times we will have proof."

Les figures it can't hurt but Lazlo's activity made him nervous.

"But you promise to help Aki right?" Les asked.

"Of course," the professor said.

"Okay," Les said.

He slipped his phone out of his pocket and opened the recent calls menu. Aki's number is dialed. The professor put the camera down to his side and Lazlo leaned into the corner. The light above flickered. The phone rang twice and was answered.

"L, these guys are lying to you," Aki said.

"What?" Les said.

Lazlo tapped the touch screen to the hand held device and the electric buzz Les heard the other day returned.

"They are lying. Leave. They want to use us. Call you later," Aki said and Les hung up.

A half-smile was clipped under the professor's now menacing stare and he held his hand out.

"He's here isn't he? Give me the phone," Professor Gluck said.

"No and what the hell is that buzzing?" Les asked.

Lazlo stepped up to the table and reached under it. The sound of Velcro releasing its grip hissed through the room over the buzz. Lazlo pulled out a hand held FLIR camera and looked through. He saw a cool blue mass seething around Les's hand and phone.

"He's in there," Lazlo said.

The phone vibrated in Les's hand.

"Answer it. It can only be your friend," Professor Gluck said.

"How'd you know that?"

"Because that buzz you hear is an electromagnetic field. We just created an energy envelope. There are high powered magnets above you, below you, and in the walls. Answer it."

Les answered the phone.

"Aki that you?" Les asked

"Yes. I'm trapped."

"What do you want me to do?" Les asked.

"I don't know. Go along with it. I don't have a lot of time left before I disintegrate though. You must get us out of here," Aki said.

"Okay," Les said.

The professor looked confused and Lazlo got closer with the FLIR camera. Les closed the phone.

"You get your recordings?" Les asked.

The professor looked at Lazlo and he nodded.

"Yes."

"You can turn the envelope off now. The buzz is giving me a headache," Les said.

"Sorry, can't do that," Professor Gluck said.

"We have it professor. Can't let it go," Lazlo said.

"Have it? You wanted to trap Aki in here all along! I'm leaving," Les said.

"But he won't be going with you. The EM barrier has him contained. You can leave but he's staying," Professor Gluck said.

A crack of lightning split the air outside and rumble of thunder followed a few seconds later. An instant later, lightning illuminated the clouds above the professor's house and snaked down through the humid air and struck the power lines. Sparks like white hot diamond chips scattered across the lawn. The house shook and dust fell from the rafters. Les looked up to the light that flickered and then it went out. The house was dark as tar.

"Screw you professor," Les said.

He pushed the table out of the way and made a straight line to where he thought the door should be. The emergency generator kicked on but Les was out the door. Lazlo and the professor followed fast as they could while Les stomped up the stairs.

In the dark living room on the way to the front door, Les turned around to see the professor following but continued on with the phone firmly in his grip.

"Les, stop. Listen to me," Professor Gluck said.

"No, you tried to trap Aki. You lied again. I'm out," Les said.

"Maybe so but it was for the greater good," Professor Gluck said.

Les yanked open the door to see low clouds tumble across the sky like boiling milk. Rain began to pour as a green hue veiled the landscape.

"Have your money back," Les said.

"No keep it. You earned it. But listen Lester, you must contact your friend again. I promise to let him go after all the proof is collected and then I will commit all my resources to helping your friend," Professor Gluck said as Lazlo stepped out in front of him ready to pounce on Les.

"How long?" Les asked.

"Just a month so I can get other experts here."

"No, I don't trust you," Les said and stepped out into the storm.

The winds slammed the door shut but the professor heaved it open and went outside. His lab coat flapped across his body in the strong wind like a loose sail.

"Les, you have to make a choice. The living or the dead. I know people where your father works at Solarian. I can have him fired with a phone call and I have you on tape admitting to what some people would call crazy ideas. The video could be posted on Youtube and how would that look? Your family would be shunned and you would be looked at as a lunatic," Professor Gluck said and a half grin appeared.

"You would do that?" Les asked.

The warm rain smeared his hair down flat on his forehead and the water dripped into his eyes.

"For science, yes. Choose. Be apart of something great or be nothing. Think about kid," Professor Gluck said.

Les picked up his roller blades behind the juniper bush and slipped them on quick.

"You fiend for the wrong things man. Get a life," Les said.

He left Professor Gluck and Lazlo on the stairs. The wind howled tossing leaves and debris about the yard. Hands up in front of his face, Les braced himself against the wind and skated away.

"So what now?" Lazlo asked.

"We follow him like planned and take the phone. One way or another we will trap the ghost in the cell."

Chapter 20: The remains.

In a bus stop sheltered by a plastic roof with walls splattered with advertisements for Broadway musicals, Les waited for the rain to thin out as it pattered on the roof. Soaked and shaken up, he watched the cars drive by as they sprayed water from roadside puddles. He needed to know so he pulled out his phone and dialed.

"We got lucky L, but I don't have much time. I only have two minutes left so I have to hurry. Help Rachel and don't worry about me anymore. Just help her," Aki said.

"Did they really trap you?"

"Yes. I was stuck. That doesn't matter anymore. Help her. We can't talk much anymore. I have to go. Bye," Aki said.

Les closed the phone and water from his scalp dripped down off the tip of his nose. He sat on the bench and listened to the downpour tapping away on the plastic roof like a toy drum. It was fresh and clean. After the next bus pulled up and then drove off leaving a puff of diesel smoke drifting along the street, the clouds broke and the rain stopped. He skated down the wet streets and wondered what he was going to do and how he would get Rachel to the city? The rain began to evaporate as a hiss of steam off the roads.

It felt strange for Les not having a hyper dog spinning at his feet when he walked through the front door. His mother turned the corner from the hall and saw him leaving a puddle on the hardwood floor by the stairs. She came back with a dish towel and tossed it to Les.

"Thanks Mom. Where's Dad?"

"Grocery store. He went to get some dried fruit. Doctor said he needed more fiber. Oh, Eddie stopped by. A set of keys and an envelope are on your nightstand. She said she'd text you tomorrow," Mrs. Logan said.

"How are you?"

"Waiting. Just waiting for Wooly to burst through and jump on the couch. How are you?" she asked.

"Still processing it. I miss him though," Les said and turned away as he dried his head with the towel.

"I do too. Go change."

Up on Les's nightstand were the keys to Biggie Blue. He recognized Eddie's Daffy Duck keychain and he opened the letter.

L,

Biggie Blue needs love so I need you to start him once a week. Drive him if you want. I trust you.

E

After a long conversation at dinner about how kids didn't get enough vitamin D and how bad the addition will look on their neighbor's house down the street, Les gave his father cash. In return, Mr. Logan gave Les his credit card. Les went online and reserved tickets for Snaggle Toothed Gauchos. He also found the other event he thought would really help restore Rachel's confidence if she agreed to do it. Les went on Facebook and posted: Going to see STG at the Palladian. Psyched. BTW don't trust men in lab coats.

. . .

On the other side of town, Lazlo intercepted the post and smiled a twisted grin as he knew that he could call Les and know exactly where he was at anytime. The professor's plan was closed to being criminal but Lazlo thought in the name of truth everything can be justified. Lazlo looked up the Palladian online and saw who Les was talking about and informed the professor.

. . .

Rachel and Les chatted via Facebook and a plan was hatched. She would tell her parents she was getting picked up to go to the transplant support group in Milton and Les said he would find a way to get them to the train. They said good night and Les texted P.J. with his plan. P.J. called and Les thought that was weird.

"Yo dude, how's being planted?" Les asked.

"Being grounded sucks. But got your text, tell me more about the deal," P.J. said.

"Basically, somehow getting her to the train, getting her to the show and then a special thing I have planned. You can't make it can you?" Les asked.

"I'm only allowed to leave during the most dire of circumstances. So no, but it looks like you have this all figured out. But if dire circumstance erupt, call me," P.J. said.

"Right on, how much do you think a cab from Clover to the train would cost?" Les asked.

"Like fifty bucks, and dude, that would be kind of obvious pulling up to her house. You know what you need to do. Eddie told me she left her keys with you," P.J. said.

"But Rachel's father would recognize me pulling up," Les said.

"Ugh. What can you do to be all stealthy ninja-like?" P.J. asked.

"I could go all celebrity by wearing sunglasses and a baseball cap," Les said.

"Sure but why not up the stakes?"

"Halloween dude. That will work."

"It's go time then. Set the plan. You have all you need. Now, just grab your balls and do it," P.J. said.

"There's one thing. That professor gig I told you about got seriously freaky. Like the guy's a demented Ghostbuster or something. He tried to trap Aki in a field," Les said.

"A field?"

"Like an electric field," Les said and sat on the edged of his bed.

"Oh, just avoid him," P.J. said.

"Dude said he'd have my dad fired if I didn't get Aki to him," Les said.

"He's bluffing. Deviant professors like that got no pull. Your dad does a good job. They won't fire him because most companies are afraid of wrongful termination lawsuits, or that's what my father says. Forget it and do what you have to. Guy's a nut job. Got to go. Text me when things begin. Bye."

"Bye."

On the bed, folded laundry smelling of fabric softener waited for Les to put it away. He opened his chest under the Rangers' banner tacked to the wall and the drawers were empty. The opportunity of space got Les thinking so he put dark shirts on one side of the drawer and light on the other. Dark socks went on one side in another drawer and white on the other. A sense of satisfaction snuck into Les after he was done and he looked at the bed. It was bare. He looked at the floor. It was bare. An ache wrenched at his heart when he realized the room was could never be as it once was. His phone vibrated on the nightstand. He checked and it was the professor. Les put the phone back down.

Sleep poured over Les like mercury out of a glass pitcher. His dreams were shiny and bright as a square sky laid flat, blue and white, in his fractured mind. The horizon was without end and so far away that it lacked depth beyond the forest of his dreams that grew with gray flowers and gray trees. A fit of howls struck Les from behind and liquid leaden clouds rolled over him. The treetops trembled with hard winds. He tried to call for help but his voice was gone. He tried to run but his feet were planted in the ground. A faceless man with a pole net stepped out from behind a tree. Les realized he was a dog with a white furry snout and the man was a dog catcher. The man ran at Les with the net held high ready to swing.

Out of the corner of Les's eye, he saw a bigger dog running at him. He gave into the moment and knew he could not win against both foes. The dog bound at Les with teeth out in a gleaming snarl. The dog then leapt over Les and stood in front of him to block the dog catcher. The bigger dog barked so loud and deep that it shook the ground and cracked the sky. A bolt of lightning crisscrossed from cloud to cloud above and struck the man with the pole net. Les's feet were free.

"Wooly," Les barked in his dream.

The big dog's tail wagged.

Les's eyes flashed open.

"Wooly," Les said to his empty room.

Outside in the hall, his mother stood by his door and heard what Les had said. Her hand went over her heart as she shook her head. Round motherly eyes began to well up with tears and she touched the door with the palm of her hand.

...

Over the next two days Rachel and Les chatted on Facebook and found that they had a lot in common starting with how it was to be an only child. P.J. and Eddie both had older sisters in college so Les never spoke about such things with them and he liked opening up to Rachel. This also helped ease Rachel's tension and worry about going to the concert, but she still wrote that she was afraid. Les told her that she'd be fine, and if she wanted, he would bring Purell to clean his hands and Lysol too.

She told Les to never mention Lysol since her whole house smelled of it. Plans were confirmed but Les had one last call to make before there was no return.

Chapter 21: A wig and a prayer.

The day came with new dry air and hope saturated every cell in Les's body. He couldn't stop scratching his knees though. They were red and ashy. Les asked his father if anything at work was troubling him right before he left. Mr. Logan shook his head, hugged his son, and told him everything was going great. That was all Les needed to hear.

Up in his room he called Eddie and sat as his computer waiting for it to boot up. The computer was slow and he wondered if it caught a worm or some new Adware that his anti-virus software couldn't find. The phone rang and rang as Les spun in his chair to look over his tidy room.

"Hey L," Eddie said.

"Hey Eddie. How's work?"

"Awesome, I got to take test photos of a Shelby Cobra and a Bugati," Eddie said.

"Those are cars right?" Les asked.

"Uh yeah, forgot you're not into cars. So you got the keys?" she asked.

Les spun back around to face his monitor and took hold of the mouse.

"I did," he said.

"If you don't want to drive BB you don't have to, but please just go and start it once a week for me until I get back. My mom will forget," she said.

"I will. So I can drive it?"

"Sure. Really? You want to drive it?" she asked.

"If I'm going to help Aki, I have to," Les said.

"Cool just don't ding BB," she said.

"I'll try. And so you know, I couldn't help Aki without you," Les said.

"Yeah you could, but thanks. I'm getting ready for today's gig at a VW car show in Berryville so I have to go. Let me know how everything turns out. I can feel it will all be just fine," she said.

"Just got to deal with it. It's been hard and a bad thing happened," Les said.

"What?" she asked.

"Wooly Bully got hit by a car. He's gone," Les said.

A long pause filled the vast space between them.

"I'm so sorry. That's horrible. Remember that Wooly Bully loved you and will be waiting when this trip through the universe is over," Eddie said.

"I hope so."

"Now go help Aki," she said.

"I will."

"Bye. Text me when you can."

"Bye."

He put then phone down and went online. Rachel sent him a message on Facebook.

Ready. 6PM my house. CU later.

Les replied

BTW, I'll B there wearing a wig.

Les went into his closet and a mound of winter clothes, sporting equipment, and garbage bags filled with his old Beanie Baby collection he was going to sell on Ebay tumbled out. He pushed the clutter to the sides as he dug for his disguise. Behind a stack of brown boxes and his Star Wars action figures, MIB, Mint In Box, he found the wig. As he pulled out the long blond wig, dust scattered and he shook it clean.

"Ugh, smells like ass and eggs," he said and tried it on.

He walked over to his dresser where a hand held mirror lay flat on top and grabbed it. The wig looked like a hay bale resting on his head so he yanked it down snug pulling it from side to side. He looked again.

"Better. Can't believe I wore this last Halloween. Looked better than P.J. in his Harry Potter gear though. Right Aki?" Les asked and looked at his phone.

"Yeah don't answer that. Better not waste minutes."

His plan was set and his disguise to infiltrate Clover ready, so Les went down stairs to talk to his mother before she left.

The breakfast nook captured the green and yellow light passing through the canopy of trees outside. His mother's coffee steamed off a thick aroma as Les sat next to her while eating Honeydew melon with a knife and fork. She looked over with a smile.

"Mom, tonight I'm going to a concert," Les said.

"Don't you think you should be asking," she asked.

"Can I?"

"Where is it?" she asked and slipped a piece of melon into her mouth.

"NYC."

"The City, oh, and who are you going with?"

"A girl I met named Rachel," Les said and looked down at the table.

"Oh I see, and how are you getting there?"

"Train."

"How are you getting to the train? I won't be home until after seven and neither will your father. Are you meeting her there?" she asked and put her knife down on the rim of her plate.

"No. She lives in Clover," Les said and looked back at his mother.

He saw her holding back a smile. He could tell.

"P.J. or Eddie going?" she asked.

"No, P.J. can't and Eddie is away. That's why she gave me her keys. She wants me to start her car once in a while and said I could drive it," Les said and straightened up.

"You're going to drive?" she asked and wiped the corners of her mouth with a napkin.

"Yup. I'm going to pick Rachel up at her house and then park at the train station."

"You have my permission then. You're old enough now, but please be careful," she said.

"Cool. And I will be. Don't worry," Les said and hugged his mother while seated.

She hugged him back harder. The embrace ended and Les took a deep breath.

"Before I go to work, would you go with me to pick up Wooly's ashes at the vet?" she asked.

"Yeah."

And so Mrs. Logan finished eating, Les got a cup of coffee, and they went to pick up the urn with Wooly Bully's remains. On the way they talked about how they almost returned the dog to the pound because he was so hyper and how he would rip up strips of sod in the backyard making Mr. Logan so upset.

The veterinary hospital was clamoring with dogs, young and old, fit and tubby, sick and those just there to get shots, as Les and Mrs. Logan walked inside with hearts weighted by solemn memory. A woman with a cat carrier stood in line at the front desk and a little gray kitty peaked out the wire door to look at Les. He waved at the kitty that mewed and poked its tiny paw out through wires. The bill was paid and Les carried the urn back out to his mother's car.

At home Les and his mother decided to scatter the ashes in the yard later on that week. His mother went to work and Les went up stairs where he found that he left his phone next to his keyboard. It was vibrating and lighting up. Les snatched the phone and saw that Professor Gluck was calling. He left a voice mail. Les listened.

"Les, make your decision. Your father loses his job and your family is disgraced with a crazy son or come be part of the greatest scientific discovery in history. It's your choice. Call me back as soon as you can," Professor Gluck's message said.

Les sent Professor Gluck a text.

…

In the professor's house on the second floor, Lazlo scanned the internet for other targets and Professor Gluck pulled out his phone.

"Ah, Les sent me text," Professor Gluck said.

Lazlo looked away from the screen and sat back in his chair. He put his hands on his head and watched the professor read the message.

"So?" Lazlo asked.

"He called our bluff."

"Is that what he said?" Lazlo asked.

"No, his reply was rather crude."

"So what do we do now?" Lazlo asked and lowered his arms.

"We know where he's going. We take the phone like I said before."

…

Across town, Les knees were on fire from itching so he went to the bathroom to put lotion on them while he waited. The hours stalled and parked like a Chevy with a seized engine spewing steam from the radiator, but finally the time came. Les grabbed the keys and slung his backpack stuffed with supplies over his shoulder. As he passed his desk, the black jewelry box with his grandfather's watch sat under a column of light.

"I got the picture man," Les said and opened the box. He slid the repaired watch with new black bands around his wrist and spun the dial.

"Time to begin again."

In the garage, Les put on his roller blades and then headed over to Eddie's house a couple miles away down the even streets and up the switchback highway.

A castaway house by a forgotten lawn, overgrown with wispy grasses and lilac, sat tilted on the slope of a hill trapped by the shade of an ancient oak. Biggie Blue was parked on the slanted street in front of the blue house with black shutters that some might call derelict. The tiny house was a footnote to Eddie's life but her mother lived there now stranded by her past. It was the size of the shed at her father's house across town in the Deerfield Pass section of New Hebron where old money played paddle ball and swam laps in over-chlorinated pools.

Les didn't see Eddie's mother around, or any other cars for that matter, so he called the home phone and left the message that he was borrowing the car for a night because Eddie said he could. He popped the trunk, took of his roller blades, slipped on his Vans and stowed his backpack. That was the easy part and now he sat in the driver's seat staring at the steering wheel. He mentally mapped out his route and knew it was five o'clock so he had an hour and a half. He could take flat, town roads instead of the highway.

Biggie Blue rumbled and revved. The front of the car dipped to the left as Les hit the gas. The engine was powerful and temperamental. He slipped the car in gear and lightly tapped the gas pedal. Biggie Blue coasted down the hill.

With his confidence building, Les changed lanes instead of waiting for a car to turn and he followed the old King's Highway, which wasn't a highway at all, through New Hebron to Milton and down to Fair Glen where he turned onto the connector that led to the Pequot reservoir in Clover. Les pulled into a lot along the deep reservoir marked Scenic View and parked.

Les scanned the lot, the horizon, and the road for passersby. He had the all clear. Out came the backpack and out came the wig. To make the illusion complete, he pulled out the polyester blouse with the black and white pattern out of the backpack. It was the very shirt he wore for Halloween the year before when he and Aki thought it would be funny to dress up as two of the girls from the Gossip Girls TV show. Les was glad he shaved the night before. On his phone he saw the time. Fifteen minutes to six o'clock. He had to motor.

After passing Rachel's road once, he turned around and found it with two minutes to spare. He texted Rachel that he would be there in ten seconds.

Exploding out the front door backwards, Rachel waved.

"Gonna be late. Can't wait. Bye," Rachel said and closed the door.

She spun around and came running with her oversized cream colored handbag with a smile from ear to ear. Her eyes were wide with the excitement that had been packed away long ago. She lugged the door open, tumbled in and turned to Les.

"Go! Go, go, go," she said and pointed forward with a sharp nod.

He jammed on the gas, but not too hard because he didn't want to screech the tires and worry her father. He might follow.

"Hi," Les said and took a firm grip of the wheel as they headed for the sun still high in the summer sky.

"You weren't kidding about the wig. You look lovely," Rachel said.

"Ha, ha. So, you ready?" Les asked.

"Hope so, got my water, took my pills this morning but brought some extra Rappamune just in case we got stuck. Cash, phone, makeup, yup, I have all I need," she said as the wind scattered her springy curls across her face.

"Cool," Les said and shot a smile at her.

"I haven't been to the city in like a year. Do we buy the tickets on the platform still?" she asked.

"Yup. Twenty-two fifty round trip. If you need any money I got you, so let's just have fun," Les said.

"You are sweet. Crazy but sweet. You want me to take that wig off? You look like a singer from an eighties metal band wearing his grandmother's blouse," she said.

Les nodded and she shimmied over in the deep front seat of Biggie Blue and wrestled the blonde wig off his head as they came to a stop a four way intersection.

"This is going to be fun," Les said.

Red soon became green.

The speed limit was observed, despite the honking horns behind them, but they reached the train station parking lot safe and on time. His hands squeezed the steering wheel tight, fingertips flattened with his grip, as they went by the spot where Les almost crashed the Fiat. Biggie Blue came to rest at the far end of the commuter lot where parking was allowed after one in the afternoon. Now, they wouldn't have to pay an orange mail in ticket that would have been stuck under the windshield wiper.

They walked up the steps to the cement platform where a green awning hung from the building and Rachel's father called. Les figured that at any moment Mr. Higgs would pop out from behind the rustic station house at any second. Rachel smiled and reassured her father that she had hand sanitizer, extra medication, and she felt fine. She ended the call and tucked the phone into her large handbag that bumped into Les's hip.

"I just need to be home before midnight but otherwise I think we're good. Sort of nervous," she said.

"An hour in and an hour back. Show starts at eight thirty, actually the opening act goes on at seven thirty, but STG takes the stage at eight thirty. Train should be here in five minutes so we'll have plenty of time to get there," Les said.

"I just hope this helps your friend," she said.

"I think we're doing that right now."

They went over to the ticket machine with the large touch screen and fed it cash for round trip tickets. Les noticed his hands were trembling a bit but not from fear.

I'm actually excited. Things might just pay off, he thought.

Chapter 22: Tracks

The commuter train's whistle blew as it hauled around the bend. Metal wheels screeched to a halt at the cement platform. Double doors slid into the aluminum body of the train right in front of Rachel and Les. They looked at each other and Les shrugged. A double row of seats facing each other just behind the partition were open so they grabbed them. Rachel faced forward and Les faced backward at the window. His knees began to itch but he resisted the impulse to scratch considering that his white shorts were just cut above the raw spots and he didn't want to get them bloody. Rachel put her right foot up on the red seat beside Les who happened to be sitting on a crack running up the surface of the shiny fake leather. Les admired her powder blue sneakers with wide white laces.

"Nice kicks," Les said.

Rachel looked down at his shoes.

"A Van's man I see," she said.

"For ages. Should be taking off soon," Les said and turned to look out the window.

The doors sealed with a gush of air and the train seemed to hop on the tracks as it shook and lumbered forward. Off by the entrance to the commuter lot, Les saw Lazlo's Prius race down to the platform through the window. He sat up straight and focused. The car came to an abrupt stop and Les saw Professor Gluck jump out of the car. He was wearing a baseball cap and a t-shirt. The professor pointed at the train and slammed his cap on the ground as they disappeared from view.

Les's heart began to beat like he was getting hit in the chest with a hockey puck over and over. Rachel noticed the worry on his face.

"What's wrong?" she asked.

"I just need to call someone. Nothing big," Les said and pulled out his phone.

"Excuse me," he said, got up and headed to the areas between the partitions and sliding doors. He dialed.

"Hey L, what's up? You on your way?" P.J. asked.

"Dude. Emergency. I need your help."

"Shoot," P.J. said.

"The professor and his assistant are following me. I told them I wouldn't help and they showed up at the train station a few seconds ago. They missed the train and the professor looked way angry," Les said.

"Okay. I'll hop the next train and follow. Don't know how but I'll be there. Get me a ticket for STG," P.J. said.

"I'll try," Les said.

"This is going to get ugly with the rents but I'll be there. Bye."

"Bye," Les said, headed back down the rocking aisle and sat.

Sweat dripped down his forehead as the AC gushed out of vent below the window. Waves of cold rippled down his back.

"Everything all right?" Rachel asked.

"I think it will be now."

...

P.J. climbed down the butterfly staircase, went to the white tiled foyer that smelled of pine, and peered through the target window to see if his father's car was there. A black Mercedes like night cut from the heavens dominated the driveway. He reached in his pocket and pulled out his overstuffed wallet. He closed his eyes as he put the wallet back.

"Gave Les my quarter," P.J. said, opened his eyes and headed to his father's study.

A pair of legs crossed at the ankles, tipped with black loafers, poked out from behind a maroon armchair as P.J looked through the study's open doorway. Light passing through the eastern window framed the feet in a square of white light. P.J. knocked on the doorframe.

"Come in," Mr. Woods said.

P.J. walked around the chair and stood in sunlight. It warmed his back in an instant.

"Father, I need to help Les so I need you to lift the ban," P.J said.

"And what do I get out of it? In all negotiations, there must be a give and take," Mr. Woods said.

"How about my unending admiration?" P.J asked.

"Amusing but I wasn't put on this earth for your admiration. I'm here to teach you how to be successful. In the business world everything is a negotiation," Mr. Woods said.

"We're going to do this now? My friend needs my help and I have to get to the city. Can we just take this day and add it on to the end of the schedule?" P.J. asked.

"That would place me in a weak position. You could just change things as you saw fit, so no. Here's a proposition. You can substitute this evening for your trip to Europe," Mr. Woods said.

P.J. stepped out of the light and went over to the bookcase smooth with leather bound editions of titles no one has read in fifty years. He ran his hand across the binding of a blue book with gold lettering.

"That's a bit drastic," P.J. said.

"Don't you see what I'm doing? I'm evaluating your interest and thus the value of what I can get in return," Mr. Woods said.

"Why does everything have to be about business with you?" P.J. asked.

"Because everything is about business and the contracts of which we are bound. Choose. Europe or go help your friend in the city?" Mr. Woods said.

"One measly night for a whole vacation. Does my homebound exile remain?" P.J. asked.

"You're not getting out of being grounded," Mr. Woods said.

"This is shit," P.J. said.

"I understand. Your choice is made. Have a nice time in the city," Mr. Woods said.

P.J walked out the door, grabbed his keys and went out the back through the screened in porch where his mother in her tennis outfit sat in a curl at the patio table. She sipped from a tall frosted glass.

"Where are you going?" she asked.

"City," P.J. said.

"I thought you were grounded?" she asked.

"Father and I negotiated," he said.

"And what did he get in return?" she asked.

"A swear, and he won the bet. I must go mother," he said.

P.J. walked over to his mother, leaned over to give her a kiss and the scent of gin and tonic spiraled up to his nose.

"Be good," he said.

"Be safe," she said and kissed him on the cheek with gin spiked lips.

The alcohol evaporated on his cheek as an outline of a cold kiss.

…

The train jostled Rachel and Les back and forth in their fake leather seats as they discussed going to college. Les was relieved P.J. was coming and felt more relaxed now that someone would have his back.

The conductor's call of "Tickets, tickets please" bounced from ear to ear until he reached Les and Rachel. The conductor looked down at them and his cap slipped forward. He held out his hand and said, "Ticket." Rachel handed her ticket to the conductor first. Tickets were punched and the conductor shuffled away down the cabin with a "Tickets, tickets please."

One thing kept popping to Les's mind and he couldn't shake the thought. It seemed impolite to ask but he had to know since the question bound to his mind long ago when he first read about transplants.

"Hey, I was wondering does the racial thing effect transplants? I mean Aki was Japanese and…" Les said and before he could spit the rest out Rachel chuckled.

"No it doesn't matter at all. We're all related if you go back far enough. Skin color is just pigment. You think hair color makes a difference?" she asked and scooted forward a bit.

"No."

"Basically it's the same thing. If you have the same blood type and a few other things work out as a genetic match, organs are organs. We all take drugs to stop from rejecting them too," she said and sat back as her chest heaved in her blouse from the train's motion. Les tried not to watch and looked to her side.

"So your heritage didn't matter. Cool," Les said.

He rubbed the top of his knees.

"Heritage? No, but I think I know what you're getting at. My mother is from Trinidad and you saw my dad, white as the Alps. That's why I have a tan year round," she said.

"Cool. Always wanted to go down to the islands but my family isn't the type that winters in St. Marten. We winter in winter," Les said and looked up to her.

"My mother hates winter. But not as much as my dad hates germs," she said.

The train screeched to a hard halt. The people by the sliding doors waiting to exit stood heavy to one side and fought the train's momentum so they wouldn't be tossed down the aisle. A sharp clamping noise rattled in the undercarriage. The door swooshed open.

A conductor announced through the intercom, "South Sanford station. Express to Grand Central from this point."

A rush of passengers flowed through the doors and filled up almost every seat. Les bowed his head and leaned forward.

"Just wondering, was your dad always so strict?" Les asked.

"Yes, but not so overbearing. They diagnosed my disease when I was a baby and had a surgery to help my liver pass bile into my digestive tract. They knew one day either I needed a transplant or would die. Things went really well until they didn't. Luckily I got a liver," Rachel said and looked at Les.

Les closed his eyes and thought about Aki during Halloween the year before.

"You okay," she asked.

"Just thinking about the guy who gave you the liver," Les said.

"Tell me more about him," Rachel said.

And so he did.

...

On the following train, thirty minutes behind, Professor Gluck and Lazlo were stuffed into a two-seater. Lazlo had his smart phone out and was playing Angry Birds. A boy with a garland of bronze hair turned around in the seat in front of them and stared at the professor. The professor rolled a finger wave at the boy. The boy put his thumbs in his ears and waved moose antlers back.

"Lazlo, can you still track Les?" Professor Gluck asked.

Four rows up by the door partition, P.J.'s ears caught the name Les out of the air filled with the background noise of the fast moving train. He turned around half way in his seat to get a view, but pretended like he was just relaxing.

"Lazlo, stop playing that. Can you still track Les from that phone?" he asked.

P.J. spotted them and turned back around in his seat.

"Yes professor. The call can be triangulated and a signal sent back to the computer in the lab. It will use the GSP coordinates and give us location. Then it will email me a map," Lazlo said.

"Their train should be getting to Grand Central Terminal soon. Call him when we arrive," Professor Gluck said.

P.J. texted Les with a description of Lazlo.

. . .

On Les and Rachel's train, Les was telling Rachel about Aki's art when his phone vibrated in his pocket. He pulled it out.

"Hold on sec. Got a text," Les said and read the text.

Les texted back a confirmation.

"So where were we? Ah, Aki's art. He was amazing. The world lost something great in him. Also, in Japan, he told me they called him an otaku, which is like saying fanboy here," Les said.

"Fanboy huh? Sounds like a great guy and I'm grateful. But I still don't really know how going to a concert will help him," she said.

"It's an indirect thing," Les said.

"Can you still talk to him?" she asked.

"Not sure there's minutes left. Crazy huh?"

"Yeah, pretty crazy. But I believe. Always have. We just have to see it through," she said and the train was covered by darkness as it entered a tunnel.

Chapter 23: NYC

Grand Central Terminal was alive with thousands of fast footsteps. Commuters, tourists, and New Yorkers alike crisscrossed paths and sped along to their destinations as Rachel and Les came to the information desk in the center of the majestic main concourse where the iconic four faced clock loomed above the crowds as a beacon to motion. It ticked and tocked to remind the people passing along the polished floors that the moments go fast. Les pointed to the Forty-Second Street exit and they walked out to a wall of wooden doors no one held open as they approached.

Out on the street they were greeted by diesel exhaust puffing out of delivery trucks, cabs honking their round horns and the smoke drifting off a street cart selling hotdogs, pretzels and sodas.

"Smells like a used match," Rachel said.

Les looked up directions to the Palladian Theatre the night before and knew his way through the grid of Midtown, but they had to venture farther down where the villages lived.

"It's like thirty or so blocks south. You feel up to walking a few blocks down Park Ave.?" Les asked.

"It's not too hot out, sure," Rachel said.

The "Walk" signal-light across Forty-Second Street lit up and the crowd at the intersection bowled over to the other side. They followed. On Park Avenue, they strolled by banks with glass walls and vendors selling flowers as they went up the gradual incline. The avenue leveled off as they reached Thirty-Ninth Street where awnings and doormen for swanky apartments held guard of the lower levels. Easels with restaurant menus dotted the sidewalk at every glass framed entrance to an eatery they slipped by.

"I was wondering. Can you dance on your medication?" Les asked.

"Sure, it only lowers my immune system so my body doesn't reject my liver," Rachel said.

"Any side effects?" Les asked as they came to stop at an intersection.

"No, not really with the new meds. At first I took Neoral-Cyclosporin and it was harsh on my kidneys so they change my meds to Rappamune. So I can dance even though I haven't, well in public, for a long time," Rachel said.

"You miss your prom?" Les asked as they began to cross the street.

"Yeah. Sucked. But, I know my parents meant well. They're just scared. I am too, but I feel good today," she said as she began to cross the intersection.

A Port Authority Bus came barreling down the street. The driver slung back a bag of Skittles and didn't notice the red light. Les turned his head just in time and hauled Rachel back up on the curb. Shouts of the pedestrians went unheard as the driver kept going and two cabs almost slammed into the side of the bus.

"You okay?" Les asked.

"Fine. What a jerk," Rachel said.

"Yeah, I forgot they don't stop sometimes. Want to take a cab?" he asked.

"Yes."

Les hailed a cab with a few hard waves. They slid in and were off downtown in a shot. Midtown fell away as the skyscrapers behind them lowered in the sky.

. . .

The professor's train slowed as it entered the dark lower levels of Grand Central Terminal, Lazlo dialed Les's number and shielded his other ear from the noise. In the cab, Les plucked his phone out of his pocket and answered.

"I know you're following me. Go away or I'll call the cops," Les said, hung up and smiled at Rachel sitting back in the cab's back seat.

In the train, Lazlo smirked and put his phone away.

"He said he knew we were following him. No matter, we know he is en route to the Palladian," Lazlo said and the professor nodded.

. . .

Standing, waiting to depart a few rows up, P.J. overheard and decided to tail the odd couple instead of racing off. When they got outside, he could text Les. The train ground to a trembling stop and the doors parted. P.J. stepped out into the underground heat, dense with scent of sour garbage, and made his way to an iron support beam in the middle of the platform. He let the swarms pass him by and pulled out his phone.

As P.J. pretended to check messages, he kept and eye out for the professor and Lazlo. Looking grumpy, the two pursuers stepped out of the train and Professor Gluck's face wrinkled with disgust from the heavy odor. He waved his hand in front of his nose and Lazlo led the way out through the hoards of shuffling bodies. P.J. stepped into the flow of commuters and followed the two up the incline to the terminal that was loud with fuzzy announcements echoing through the grand expanse.

...

Behind a purple velvet rope, Les and Rachel stood in line at the Palladian Theatre. The sidewalk bustled with foot traffic. The city, vivid with color, loud as a yell, was an unending procession of humanity in all shape and sizes. Les turned to Rachel who held her handbag across her stomach with a tight grip.

"Having fun yet?" he asked.

"Besides almost getting killed, actually, I am," she said and leaned over and kissed Les on the cheek.

His peach of a face transformed into a cherry.

"Thank you," she said.

"Oh, you're welcome. I wish we met some other way than this," Les said.

"It is what it is. One thing I wanted to ask you. When you talked to Aki, you said there were only minutes left to talk, like on cell phone?" Rachel asked.

The line moved a big chunk forward so they closed the space.

"Yup. He called me on a cell and that's what he told me. We only have a minute left, so after this is all done, I guess he'll call me," Les said and he felt his phone vibrate in his pocket.

"Excuse me," he said and pulled out the phone.

It was a text from P.J.

L, Following them. Find U there.

Les put his phone away and forced a smile.

"My friend is going to meet us," he said.

"Cool. Not looking forward to the frisk," she said.

"The pat down sucks for guys. It's like the security is trying to be all tough. Going through your bag has got to suck though," he said.

"It does. Hey, look up," she said.

Above them the marquis pulsed with a faint glow growing stronger. The marquis read Snaggle Toothed Guchos.

"That's reckless funny. Guchos," Les said.

A man with a yellow staff shirt and a ladder broke through the line with a pole in his hand and set up right in front of Les and Rachel. He put up the letters that spelled SOLD OUT.

"Looks like my friend P.J. is scalping," Les said.

The man with the ladder bullied his way back through the line and through the entrance to the theatre. Rachel nodded in the direction of the curb where two men in oversized sunglasses perched.

"Bet those are scalpers right there. As soon as the sign went up they walked to the curb," she said.

"P.J. will find tickets. But, I'll text him anyway. C'mon the line's moving," Les said.

They made it to the glass doors where they could see people being checked by security and getting their tickets ripped as they passed through metal detectors. To the other side was the Box Office, the line at the reserved ticket window was short. They saw space open up so they went in and nudged their way, foot by inch, to the Box office. Les texted P.J. the news as they waited.

…

P.J. got the text as he followed Lazlo and the professor out on to Lexington Avenue where the professor looked disoriented. Lazlo stepped to the edge of the sidewalk, flailed his arms, and whistled. A cab stopped and they got in.

"Damn it, sold out and now this," P.J. said and stepped to the curb.

The professor's cab pulled out into the fast moving traffic. P.J. held his hand out and cabs just drove by. Buses puttered bellowing hot fumes, a bicycle messenger almost tagged P.J. in the arm with his handlebar but he ducked as he zipped by and a young man with strong legs raced over on a passenger tricycle with a seat for two attached to the bicycle frame. He stopped.

"Where you going?" the man asked.

"Palladian. How fast can you get me there?" P.J. asked.

"Downtown eh, uh maybe twenty," he said.

"Not quick enough. I need a cab," P.J. said.

"Subway is the fastest way right now. Traffic going down is bad," the man said and pedaled away.

P.J. didn't like the subway. He had a bad experience as a kid when he saw a Three Card Monty hustler get into a fight with a mime. Undaunted by memory, P.J. found a staircase that descended below street level to the subway line that followed Lexington Avenue downtown. The stone steps took him into the highest level of the underworld living beneath the towers of Midtown. The scent of urine got stronger the deeper he went and he checked his phone app to see if he was on the right subway line. He was and pulled out the yellow MetroCard his father gave him a year ago.

P.J hadn't used his card in a while and it took a few swipes at the turnstile before the payment registered. He hopped on the subway. P.J was squished between a woman reading from a Kindle and a man with a brown wool cap who smelled of blue cheese, garlic and vodka.

...

The opening band played as Rachel and Les made their way to the balcony seats. He wasn't impressed with the band but Les thought Eddie would like their Psycho Billy style. They sat. The seats were soft but worn.

"You like these guys?" Rachel asked.

"Not really but I respect what they do. Got to be tough getting on stage and playing your heart out to people who aren't there to listen to you," Les said.

"It's hard. Real hard. I used to play in band," Rachel said.

"You get stage fright?"

"Fright, no, terror yes. But once the first song is done it all gets better unless you screw up. That's the worst especially if you haven't been practicing enough," she said.

"Oh," Les said and thought maybe he better rethink his alternate plan if this one failed.

...

P.J. climbed the stairs up to street level and began to walk as fast as he could toward the theatre. Some stragglers stood outside and the foot traffic was thick in the thin heat of the evening. P.J. made it to the theatre's block and saw the Professor and Lazlo walk under the marquis. He looked up and saw that the show was indeed SOLD OUT.

The clamor of horns honking and random people shouting tickled P.J.'s sensibilities and he thought that after college he had to live in Manhattan. He got to the glass doors and saw the professor and Lazlo at the Box Office being handed tickets. A security guard in black stood as still as boredom, arms crossed, in front of P.J.

"Sold out?" P.J. asked.

"That's what the sign says," he said.

"Damn."

P.J. went on the hunt for tickets. The scalpers were easy prey but they were also predators.

Chapter 24: A pocket of pick.

The balcony seethed with shadows and the voices of people singing off key to the first Snaggled Toothed Gauchos tune *Bola Love*. Les and Rachel moved to the beat and leaned over the railing to see the band dressed up like Argentine cowboys, flat rimmed Campero hats and all. Les felt a presence at his back. He spun around but his eyes couldn't penetrate the darkness.

The first song ended with a deep rolling cheer as the guitarist let the last note fade away. Rachel looked at Les with a smile while she clapped and for a moment happiness covered the ache in his heart. The house lights came up and then all went black. A strobe light from the stage scanned back and forth across the crowd below Les and Rachel. The band erupted with a series of speedy notes that ripped off into the atmosphere and jumped through the crowd. They played a new song off their upcoming album that got the audience bouncing to a reggae rhythm. The lights pulsed in time with the upbeats. Rachel rocked her head to the music and Les tapped the railing when a hand slammed onto his shoulder. He turned ready to defend himself.

P.J. stared back from the two empty seats behind them. Les shook his head and then grabbed P.J. in a bear hug. Rachel stopped and looked.

"Scared the hell out of me. Glad you found us," Les said over the music.

"Everything good Rock Star?" P.J. asked.

"It's all good. This is Rachel," Les said and the embrace broke.

P.J. extended his hand to Rachel.

"Hi," she said and took his hand.

"I'm P.J. and you must be the lovely Rachel," P.J. said and shook her hand.

A flirty grin angled across her face with a charm that Casanova would have found amusing.

"Yeah, this is the guy I told you about. He knows all about the story. He helped too," Les said.

"Yup, and I'm very happy to meet you. Now, let's have fun. I spent way too much on my ticket not to," P.J. said.

The three of them let the music take them and forgot about who they were, who their parents were, and let the worries wait.

For a few songs, they were just kids at a concert, in the city, on their own.

Intermission came and the house lights came up. Les stretched and surveyed the balcony from corner to corner. A few couples were making out and some guys with ragged hair looked like they fell asleep slumped in their seats. Les nodded to P.J.

"Think those dudes behind you are spent?" Les asked him.

P.J. looked over his shoulder.

"Finished. Drunk as a stock broker," P.J. said.

"I'm going to the bathroom," Rachel said.

"I'll go down with you. I'm going to grab a drink. Coming?" Les asked P.J.

"No, I'm good. I'll protect your seats. God knows where mine even are. Lucky these no shows were right behind you," P.J. said.

"Cool."

The crowd flooded the hallways and gilded staircases of the elegant theatre. Bodies were face to face, back to front, and they clogged the paths to the bathrooms and concession area. Rachel and Les pushed through and made their way down to the ground level. With her handbag tight in her grip, she pointed with her other hand towards the sign to the bathroom.

"You got my number. Text me if you need me," Les said and she nodded.

Les went right and she went left at the bottom of the stairs. He passed by a merchandise table selling t-shirts, key chains and glossy posters on his way to the concessions stand. The line for drinks was longer than the line they waited in outside. Every millimeter was precious and Les guarded it as pockets of people just stood around outside of the lines. He focused on what was in front of him and when space opened up he took it.

Les tilted his head up and looked over the people in front of him to the menu board. He was glad he brought a good amount of cash since water was five bucks and Red Bull was ten. The cluster of people to his side got closer. He could feel the heat of their bodies radiating with salty body odor like hot ocean water. He stood his ground and worked his way forward.

Les felt hands going into his pockets, but not his own, and there was only enough space for him to turn his head. He looked to see Lazlo's almond eyes looking back. Les slammed down his arms and hit Lazlo's hands out of his pockets.

"Get off. This guy is trying to steal my wallet. Security," Les yelled at the top of his lungs.

A clearing formed, a circle opened up, and Les pushed Lazlo into it as two security guards crashed through the crowd. One with an earpiece connected to a clip-on radio grabbed Lazlo who tried to flee and the other one grabbed Les. Lazlo resisted and was put in a reverse choke.

"Who's the thief?" asked the security guard grabbing Les's shoulders.

"That dude tried to pick my pocket," Les said.

A guy with a CAT cap beside the security guard holding Les said, "That dude you got in the hold tried to take this guy's stuff. Saw him put his hands in his pockets."

"Really?" the guard asked.

"True enough bro. That dude's a thief," the guy said.

Lazlo squirmed so the guard squeezed a little tighter with his stone cut forearms and he started on a journey to dreamland as his eyes bulged with tiny red spots from the broken capillaries.

"You want us to call the cops or toss him?" the guard asked Les.

"Toss him. Getting the cops here would suck," Les said.

"All right."

Les watched as Lazlo was not so much tossed as he was dragged and placed outside on the metal grate of a closed storefront next door. He appeared to be out cold.

Les made his way back upstairs, shaken but no longer frightened, and plopped down in his seat.

"Your face is red. What'd you do jumping jacks or something?" P.J. asked.

"No, that creepy dude Lazlo found me. Tried to take my phone I think," Les said.

P.J. sat up in the seat and then leaned over.

"What happened?" P.J. asked.

"Security tossed him," Les said.

"Good. One down at least and that weak looking professor probably won't mess with us now. You know, cowards like company or that's what my father says," P.J. said.

"No worries. The plan is working and what good would it do if the professor got my phone anyway?" Les asked.

"Don't know. There she is," P.J. said.

Rachel slid down the row of seats with her bag across her chest. She was sweating.

"You okay?" Les asked.

"I'm all right. I think. Just a little weak. I better sit for a bit," she said.

"If you feel better and want to go sneak down to the stage let me know," P.J. said to Rachel.

"Thanks, but no. I haven't been in a crowd in along time. Think I'm getting claustrophobic and tired. Maybe it wasn't a good idea to do this?" Rachel said.

Les's heart collapsed. Doubt filled the space in his chest. He wasn't sure if the plan would succeed now and it could all be for nothing but P.J. popped up.

"I'm going to get you a Vitamin Water," P.J. said to Rachel.

"No you don't have to," she said.

"I insist. You'll be fine. You'll see," P.J. said and slipped away.

"Your friend is really, what's the word, dashing. Does he have a girlfriend?" Rachel asked.

"I'm asked that question all the time. I mean like all the time. And no he doesn't but, never mind, you should ask him yourself. He loves to talk about his love life," Les said.

"Oh, don't get me wrong, he's really good looking but just not for me. I have a few girls who might be interested in him though," Rachel said.

"I'm sure they'll love him. They all do. But I'll let you two talk about that. Believe me, it'll be an interesting conversation but now the band's coming on," Les said and the lights dimmed as the band sauntered on stage.

The Snaggle Toothed Gauchos played and Les and Rachel moved to the music in their seats. After the first song was over P.J. returned with a bottle of Vitamin Water and gave it to Rachel.

"Thanks," she said.

"You're welcome. Having fun?" P.J. asked.

"Oh yes," she said.

"Of course you are. You're a young woman in the city seeing a show and helping out us sad fools," P.J. said with a wink.

Rachel laughed and sipped. She began to bounce as the music picked up pace and the lightshow flashed through the dark space. A disco ball was then lowered from the rafters and hung even with the balcony's railing. The silver reflections raced in a broken geometry across the entire theatre.

The show ended with an encore and applause that didn't stop until Les, Rachel and P.J. got outside. They walked over by an alley to let the throngs of other concert goers pass.

"Have a good time?" Les asked.

"Crazy fun," P.J. said.

"Haven't had this much fun in years. I just hope this somehow helps your friend Aki cross over," Rachel said.

"I know it did. Aki just wanted you to start living. That's all," Les said.

"Now I just have to find the strength to deal with my parents," she said.

"I have something in mind," Les said and felt his phone vibrate.

He took it out expecting the call to be from his mom or the professor. It was Aki.

"Aki," Les said.

Rachel looked shocked and stepped back. P.J.'s eyes flared.

"Hey Aki, we did it. You saying good bye?" Les asked.

"Not yet, it's not over. There are a couple things you have to do. One get Bob fixed, two take Rachel to Finnegan's. It's a few blocks north. And you have one more thing to do... Wait. Let me talk to him," Aki said.

"Who? P.J.," Les asked.

"No, him," Aki said and Les turned around.

The professor stood there with Lazlo who had a red ring around his neck and his arms crossed as tight as his narrow eyes.

"He wants to talk to you," Les said to the professor.

Professor Gluck bound over and snatched the phone with an eager hand and put then phone to his ear.

"Hello, Akihide Kubo," Professor Gluck said.

P.J. widened his stance and looked at Les.

"Why?" P.J. asked.

"Aki wanted to talk to him," Les said.

"Okay. If he wants to," P.J. said.

Rachel watched the professor's face sink and posture go slack. Professor Gluck took the phone away from his ear and began to hand it over to Les with a blank stare. Lazlo jumped at the phone.

"We need this proof. I'm not starting over," Lazlo said as he grasped at the phone.

Les stepped fast to snatch the phone from the professor's hand, but Lazlo's arms swung out and hit the professor's arm sending the phone flying in an arc to the sidewalk. The phone hit the concrete and shattered into pieces as it scattered. Les rushed over, knelt down, and huddled over the remains. He started scooping up the bits of the phone as Rachel and P.J. rushed over. They stood guard over Les.

With the broken phone pieces in one hand, Les stood up on strong feet and pointed at the professor.

"By the way, threaten my family again and you'll regret it. And you're buying me a new phone jerk off," Les said.

The professor stared at the ground, shifting his weight from foot to foot in a loose wobble, and sighed.

"I'll pay for the phone. Lazlo, it's over. Everything. Can't do this research anymore," Professor Gluck said.

"We can't give up Professor. We can't," Lazlo said.

His face lifted with a slow rate and revealed eyes hard with fear.

"No, I'm not and I advise you not to. The spirit told me something. Something I cannot repeat. There are things humans aren't ready to know. Come on. Les send me a bill for the phone," Professor Gluck said and disappeared into the bustling foot traffic. Lazlo followed.

"What was that about?" P.J. asked.

Les looked at the pieces of the broken phone in his hand and Rachel put her arm around his shoulder.

"I guess we'll never know. But Aki had one last request. He wanted us to go to a place called Finnegan's up the street. I planned to go to this Karaoke bar near Grand Central but he wants us to go here," Les said.

"Karaoke, what did you have planned?" Rachel asked.

"Just fun," Les said

"No time to go to both places," P.J. said.

"Off to Finnegan's then," Les said.

They came to Finnegan's door and heard an acoustic guitar being strummed inside the Irish pub. Les shrugged and opened the door for P.J and Rachel. They slipped in a cozy booth by the guitar player in black who sat on a bar stool next to a music stand and two microphones. One microphone was for the guitar and the other was higher up so he could sing. He finger-picked a country melody as the waitress came over. They ordered Buffalo wings and listened to gentle guitar playing a soft song of melancholy. The guitar stopped and they clapped.

"Hi there. I'm J. Joyce and that song was called *Wake*. Here's the time in the set where I ask people if they'd like to come up and join me. Any brave souls out there?" J. Joyce asked.

Les shook his head yes as a revelation hit him and then looked at Rachel.

"You need to sing. That was actually what I had in store for Karaoke because I knew you were a singer in band. You know, you can regain your confidence, get your voice back. I think that's why Aki told us to come here," Les said.

"I haven't practiced and I don't know his songs," Rachel said.

"Hey J.J. what songs you got for a soprano?" P.J. asked.

"I know some Heart tunes, some Tori Amos, and Fleetwood Mac," J. Joyce said.

"Well," P.J. said to Rachel.

"I know *Landslide*," she said.

"J.J., sorry to be a bother but do you know *Landslide*?" P.J. asked.

"A favorite of mine. Why you want to sing it?" J. Joyce asked.

P.J. wagged his finger at him and scoffed a playful scoff.

"You can do it Rachel," Les said.

"But I haven't prepared or practiced," she said.

"Sometimes you just risk it. It's what life is. Please sing. I know you'll do great," Les said.

"Okay," she said and slid out of the booth.

J. Joyce began to fingerpick the Fleetwood Mac song and Rachel, right on time, sang the opening line. The guitar rose and fell and Rachel's voice climbed. Each pitch and peek note, she hit with a sultry inflection and every one in the restaurant looked in her direction.

The song came to rest and the patrons clapped. Rachel's face brightened, the edge of fear was gone, and she walked back over to the booth as the wings were being served. She hugged P.J. and then Les who hugged her back. The sadness and guilt that once lingered in Les's mind and body slipped away.

"Thanks Les. I'm not letting anything hold me back now. Weird, I smell hotdogs."

"Me too. I can smell them over these wings," Les said.

"What are you talking about?" P.J. asked and dipped a stick of celery into a spot of ranch dressing floating next to the pile of red hot wings.

"Nothing. Tell you later," Les said and knew is was Aki's way of saying good bye.

Chapter 25: Con man.

Les and Rachel kept in touch over the summer and the autumn came with a finality that one could feel with the cooler air. Rachel was taking classes at Upton College for the fall semester and Les's senior year was going fast. There was no sign of the professor anywhere. Some rumors at the college said he became a monk while others said he accidentally zapped his brain with a device and was stuck in a sanitarium in Colorado where he thought he was an orange. Neither was true but neither was entirely false either.

One Friday after classes got out, Les asked Arden to go hang out before going to work at the new coffee shop in the center of town. He drove her up to the Cascades in the Fiat with the top down. They got to know each other under the changing leaves.

Les and Arden tried to make it work but Les couldn't shake the thought of Rachel singing that night. When he looked at Arden, he saw her. The other thing he couldn't shake was that Aki had said 'one more thing' and he never got to know what that was. Even though he talked to a ghost, this was the first time he felt haunted. One day after school, his letter from SVA came.

Les went to his room, small piles of clothes dotted the landscape, and he plopped on to the edge of his bed that was neatly made with a Star Wars comforter. The envelope gave him a bit of trouble but in the end it tore. Les scratched his knees through his jeans and he could feel his pulse in his hands.

"We regret to inform you. Damn."

Later that week P.J. and Eddie sent texts telling him they got early admission to their first choice school and Les's plans for the world changed. Les figured he might not get to be an artist but he can at least go to the New York ComicCon and have a bit of closure to his youth. He thought if he had just drawn a little more that the samples he submitted would be better but that was behind him.

The weekend of the New York ComicCon came and Les packed up his new Ipad that was loaded with the sequential art work Aki and he did for the Janus Chiaroscuro comic concept. He was bringing it just in case he ran into a few guys he met in the Facebook Comic Book Creator group he joined a few weeks ago. His iPhone was secured in his pocket. Les put Bob the Gundam robot model and his old phone in his backpack. He said goodbye to his parents as the Fiat was warming up in the driveway. For some reason, he ran up to his room and grabbed Wooly Bully's collar. He just felt he needed to. The collar was looped around a backpack strap and jingled with memories as he walked to the car.

Down the even streets he drove with the top down. A few days of warm weather were left for the suburbs. He stopped at P.J.'s house and ran up to the door. Mrs. Woods answered in her white robe.

"Hi Mrs. Woods. Is P.J. here?" he asked.

"He's sleeping," she said.

"Oh, could you give him this. I don't need it anymore. Bye," Les said and handed her the lucky quarter. She waved good bye as he pulled away.

Les drove down the highway and on the roadside the houses got closer together as more cars clustered together in traffic. The land of trees gave way to the land of stone and steel.

He made good time to New York and was on the West Side Highway much faster than he thought. Cabs cut him off and traffic got congested but Les and the Fiat didn't fall apart. To his right, he came upon the aircraft carrier the USS Intrepid docked in the Hudson. Poised on top were war planes from various eras. Les was amazed by the jet fighters and knew he was at Forty Sixth Street because he had gone to the floating museum when he was in middle school.

Smoke and steam poured out of a cab's hood that had broken down on the shoulder and Les saw a hefty man wearing cargo shorts, glasses, and Adidas standing behind it holding a bag with the Uncanny Comics logo. The man was on his phone with an exhausted look scrawled across his face so Les pulled over. He got out of the car and walked up to the man who took of his glasses to wipe them on his short sleeve button down shirt.

"Hey man, going to Javits for the con?" Les asked.

The man put his glasses back on and looked Les up and down.

"Yeah," the man said.

"Want a ride?" Les asked.

"That'd be great."

"I'm Les."

"Nice to meet you."

Les was too busy concentrating on driving to start up a conversation and traffic started to move quick. In a few minutes, a sign for the Jacob Javits Convention Center made Les smile. It was the home of the New York ComicCon. They took Thirty-Forth Street to Eleventh Avenue. After some searching, the man directed Les to a parking garage on West Thirty-Seventh Street.

When Les and the man with the cargo shorts and glasses came out of the parking garage, the man turned to Les who was cinching up his backpack tight.

"You know I'm so sorry for not introducing myself. I'm D.B. Dubrowski," he said.

"Sounds familiar. Hey, you grow up around New Hebron?" Les asked.

"No way! I lived in Fair Glen. But that was like almost twenty years ago," D.B. said.

"Nice, love Pawley's," Les said.

"Best hotdogs in the state. Speaking of dogs, what's with the collar? Some sort of Cosplay thing you doing at the Con?" D.B. asked.

"No, just a luck thing. It was my dog's," Les said.

"Uh, past tense, sorry," D.B said.

"That's cool. You didn't know," Les said and they began to walk down Eleventh Avenue.

They came up to the main entrance of the massive convention center crowned with glass collecting the sun of the warm autumn morning. People were lined up outside the wall of doors as Javits Center staff in yellow shirts stood guard at the roped off entrances. Les started to walk to the end of the line when he saw that D.B. stopped. He pulled out an Exhibitor's badge on a red cord and looped it around his neck.

"Hey Les, this is where we part for now. I'm going to be at the Uncanny booth in between ten and noon. Stop by after and I'll buy you lunch," D.B. said.

"You work for Uncanny?"

"Everyday, every moment," D.B. said.

"I'll come by," Les said.

"Cool."

D.B. walked over to a glass door and flashed his laminated badge to the staff member in yellow. The man bowed and opened the door for him. Les went to wait in line and as he walked to the end he saw people dressed as characters from manga, American comics, TV and movies. He really liked the guy in the Predator costume and a kid with spiked red hair and huge curved sword dressed up as Ichigo Kurosaki from Bleach. As Les reached his spot in line, he saw grown men dressed as Jedi from Star Wars fighting with wood swords painted blue and green. In that moment, the queue cheered. Entry had begun but the lined moved slowly as if it feed on eagerness and hadn't eaten for eons.

The convention floor was huge and Les snapped pictures with his phone and posted them on Facebook and Twitter just like ten thousand others. The first order of business was to find Bob the Gundam replacement parts and he found a vendor with everything he needed. Then Les walked back and forth along Artist Alley for what seemed like miles and checked out some sketches and original art work.

His feet ached after the third hour and there was just too much too see in one day so he found a hallway where others were sitting against the wall. He kicked back and loosened the laces to his shoes. The only thought that came to his mind was that he wished Aki was there.

Noon struck. Les made his way to the Uncanny Comics booth and it was swamped with people trying to get signatures from writers and artists. He didn't see D.B. so he paced the line and then he saw him come out from behind a white backdrop curtain.

"Hey D.B." Les said.

"Hey Les. Perfect timing. I need to get out of here for a moment. Follow me."

They passed through the crowds and it seemed that a few people carrying laptops were close behind them.

"Uh D.B., I think those dudes are trailing us," Les said.

"Yup, don't worry about them," he said.

In the food court, D.B. bought Les a beef and bean burrito. They grabbed a table and Les saw the guys with laptops leaning on the wall watching them through the lines of people swarming through the corridor.

"So Les. What's your story? Fanboy, freak, collector, creator?" D.B. asked.

"My friend and I started to make comics but he died almost a year ago," Les said.

"Sorry to hear. That's rough. So, you write, pencil, ink, letter?" D.B. asked.

"I wanted to write and pencil but my friend Aki was a better artist so I don't know," Les said.

"Aki Kubo from New Hebron? My mom sent me link to a newspaper article that covered his car accident. I remember because his father is a fairly famous graphic designer. He worked on a lot of novel covers for the New York publishing houses," D.B. said.

"Yeah that was him. Aki was more talented than his father. I know, I saw both of their work," Les said.

"Very sad. So you want to pencil? You're a bit young yet. You going to school for it?" D.B. asked.

"I wanted to go to SVA but didn't get in," Les said.

"Really, you got any work on you?" D.B. asked.

"Some," Les said.

"Pull it out," D.B. said.

Les slipped out his iPad, pulled up his work, handed it to D.B., and sat back to wait for disappointment. D.B. examined the comic book panels with keen eyes tempered by years of dealing with sensitive artists, who on occasion needed therapy more than work.

"This is really good. You didn't break the borders. You articulate the hands well and the proportions are good. You need to work on linear perspective a bit and need to refine a few things like scene anatomy but SVA would be crazy not to take you. Did you send this as a sample?" D.B. asked.

"No, but it's too late now," Les said.

"No it's not. A few spot open up every semester. You are graduating from high school this summer right?" D.B. asked.

"Yes."

"You know what? Uncanny offers a partial scholarship to develop talent and they would be crazy not to take you if you had the scholarship," D.B. said.

Les pushed his chair back, rubbed his forehead and looked at D.B.

"What do you mean? Who are you?"

"See those guys waiting for me, the ones who followed us, they're artists waiting for me to tell them what I think about their portfolios. I hire artists for Uncanny among my many other jobs. And one of them is developing talent and you got it kid," D.B. said.

"No way," Les said.

"Much way. If you want the scholarship, I can get it for you and put in a good word with the dean of admissions at SVA. We go way back," D.B. said.

"Sure. I'll take it. Thank you. Thanks," Les said.

"Don't need to thank me. Your work is good Les. I wouldn't just give a scholarship away to someone just because they were nice and gave me ride. Here's my card," D.B. said and slipped a card out of his wallet.

"Thanks," Les said.

"Give me a call next week. We'll get you in and maybe when I'm home visiting we can go grab a dog at Pawley's. Cool?"

"Cool."

"I got to go do my job now. And thanks for the ride. See you around," D.B. said and waved as he walked away.

Les sat low in the chair and put his hands over his face. He wanted to laugh but his eyes welled up. He wiped them with the back of his hands and felt his phone vibrate. The iPhone was lodged in his pocket pretty tight so he had to stand up to free it. He saw the number and fell back into the seat. It was Aki's number. He answered it.

"So now I can really move on," Aki said.

"But I thought. How? What?"

"I got an extra minute credited. One call from the bright side to let you know something. Dude, you did it. You faced your fear and helped people just like I knew you would. One last request, get Janus published when you get out of SVA and remember me," Aki said.

"How could I forget," Les said.

"FYI, the adventure was about helping Rachel, but it was more about helping you. And luckily we got some help. You know when I was trapped in the professor's lab, I never would have made it to the bright side unless the power went out. Thing is, the lightning strike was a gift from a friend of yours. A guardian spirit more powerful than you can image. And, he wants to say hello. With that, I say good bye my friend. I'll see you later and I love you bro," Aki said.

"Love you to Aki," Les said.

"Tell P.J. and Eddie I said good bye."

"I will," Les said.

"Say hello to our guardian. Here he is," Aki said.

"Woof!"

"Wooly Bully!"

...

Years later, after Les graduated from SVA, he sat behind a foldout table at Midtown Comics in Manhattan. He stared at the stairs leading to the first level and tapped the tabletop with a silver Sharpie pen.

No one is going to come and it's only a couple minutes to the signing, he thought.

Exactly one minute later, pounding footsteps spiraled up the staircase and shook the floor beneath Les. A line of people rushed towards him with Issue Number One of Janus Chiaroscuro in their hands.

"We did it," Les said.